Andrew Joron

BSE

ISBN: 978-1-7363248-7-5

BSE Books are distributed by
 Small Press Distribution
 1341 Seventh Street
 Berkeley, CA 94710
 orders@spdbooks.org | www.spdbooks.org
 1-800-869-7553

BSE Books can also be purchased at
www.blacksquareeditions.org and www.hyperallergic.com

Contributions to BSE can be made to
 Off the Park Press, Inc.
 976 Kensington Ave.
 Plainfield, NJ 07060
 (Please make checks payable to Off the Park Press, Inc.)

To contact the Press please write:
 Black Square Editions
 1200 Broadway, Suite 3C
 New York, NY 10001

An independent subsidiary of Off the Park Press, Inc.
Member of CLMP.

Publisher: John Yau
Editors: Ronna Lebo and Boni Joi
Design & composition: Shanna Compton

Cover art: Brian Lucas, *Baked Atom* (24 × 19 inches, mixed media on paper)

To the early Space Age—

The Given Earth

1

Pi is a constant.
—old Terran saying

Two old men sat at a gaming board in a large room that resembled a candlelit cave. The men were twins; each might have been playing against himself in a mirror. According to the rules of the game, their moves were symmetrically reversed and simultaneous: Mike advanced a game piece with his left hand, while Ike, with his right, withdrew his piece by an equal measure. And yet, despite this mirroring, the pieces on the board shifted into new, never-recurring patterns.

The door at the far end of the room opened, and Windy the Legless Girl drifted in, her skirts fluttering over the bare floor. Windy was a casualty of the battles that had culminated in the Redefinition of Life many years ago. Her face, scarred but agelessly youthful, showed concern mixed with mild consternation. "Mike and Ike, cease your randomizing! The Screaming Satellite ascends over the *plateaux* of fused glass!"

Mike and Ike, who both had refused Redefinition, turned toward Windy with some irritation. They spoke together: "What do we care for news, no matter how dire? The game tells us all we need to know. Only when the patterns finally repeat will we rise from this table."

Windy stopped, hovering speechless. She knew they hated each other as much as they hated the outside world. They wanted to die playing the game, meditating upon the chaos patterns produced by their relentless, oddly ineffective stratagems. What news could be relevant to them, cloistered within their polygonal palace, even if it pertained to the evacuation of the city?

All at once, the air shuddered darkly—inside? outside?—as if the Earth itself had uttered a deep subsonic syllable. The twins started up from their gaming table, alarmed at last—not by news of the satellite, but by some apparently conclusive configuration of their game pieces. Yet Windy saw only the same random scatter of stones upon the board.

Now the twins walked backward, miming furiously, toward a stairwell on the opposite side of the room. Their gait was strange, as if they went—halting and faltering—feeling their way through extra, unseen dimensions of space. First they bent away from each other, then fell together awkwardly, as if seeking not to go around, but to *pass through* one another. Windy wondered, not for the first time, if Mike and Ike had once constituted two halves of a single entity, one that had been split apart by the Redefinition. Were the twins then as redefined as she was? Windy watched them for a moment, then abruptly whirled out of the room.

Outside, a crowd was gathering in anticipation of the satellite's ascension. Windy swept through the halls of the Polygon, issuing orders to the servants as she passed the kitchens and ritual chambers. "Load the carriages," she cried. "Prepare to evacuate to the Northern Refuge!" The servants, bald and beetle-like, scurried about in response. Windy had run the household ever since her adoption by the twins in the aftermath of Redefinition. Considering the twins' importance in the community, Windy, who often stood in for her reclusive guardians at city ceremonies and council meetings, had by now attained the status of a community leader. It was said that the Mind of Oopolis itself consulted with her at certain bifurcations of the Story.

Did this moment represent such a bifurcation? Opening the great portal of the Polygon, which fronted on the city square, Windy surveyed the crowd that had gathered. The sun, radiating blackness to her redefined eyes, was setting just as the satellite was rising over the opposite horizon. Something about this symmetry nagged at her. Where had the twins gone? She, along with the crowd below, could already "hear" via brain radio the high-pitched ululation of the satellite's signal.

Someone in the crowd spotted her as she swayed in midair, red robes rippling, at the top of the Polygon's stairs. "Oh Windy!" Others, seeing her there, took up the shout. "Oh Windy!"

Another scene superimposed itself on her vision: the interior of the Council Room. Behind the circle of seated councilmembers, the crowd, surging, anxious, remained faintly visible to her. She blinked, disconcerted by this double image: the faces of the city's elite hung like lamps over the dark roil of aroused citizenry. The Mind of Oopolis had tapped her into the council meeting without announcing her.

"What is the nature of this emergency?" one of the councilmembers was asking.

"The sky has been breached, in several places, by ovoid objects transmitted from the Moon," the Mind, invisible, omnipresent, replied. "Most burned up entering our atmosphere. However, two of these objects have survived their descent, coming to rest among the dust-seas to the south of the city."

"Objects from the Moon!" The councilmembers could hardly hide their disbelief. Millennia ago, long before Redefinition, the population of the Moon had renounced all contact with Oopolis, Earth's last citadel. The reasons were disputed, open to multiple and conflicting interpretations: had the Moon-people feared infection by the nanoplague that had devastated Earth's biosphere? Perhaps they were right to do so, some asserted, for the plague had eventually given rise to—

Night flashed white across Windy's vision, obliterating her view of the council. The sun had set, as if, she thought pathetically, it had wanted to escape the situation. She too wanted to escape—but from what, exactly? In the square, the crowd had fallen silent, supplicating the tiny black spark of the satellite with open hands. The Screaming Satellite's message could not be unscrambled; it had reverted to its most basic mode, reciting a litany in SPRACH, the eons-old global babel in use at the time of its launch.

"We must locate the Moon-eggs and destroy them!" This from the Generalissimo who commanded the city's rusted, mostly inoperative robot battalions. Windy replied impulsively: "Better first to observe them, and try to learn what their coming here portends." The councilmembers peered around the room: "Who said that?" Realizing that she may have violated the Mind's protocols, Windy floated back into the doorway of the Polygon, as if to hide from everyone's attention.

"Why, Windy, of course," the Generalissimo said drily. "She has become the Mind of O's favorite advisor; no doubt she joins us here by the Mind's invitation."

Now the satellite, as it rose higher, shifted modality. The SPRACH transmission ended and a set of "musick" began. Somehow the satellite had accessed a sound file from an ancient archive: a loud trumpet brayed, then another, then another, all intertwining one inhumanly prolonged note. The Generalissimo, no fan of "musick," nevertheless identified the tune: "A call to arms!" The Mind demurred: "No, it's the opening track from *Dronin' with the Esquimaux*. Never thought I'd hear that again."

One of the savants who attended council had been busy with a blue crayon, drawing spirals and arrows across a flickering wall screen. "I have deciphered an entire grammatical clause from the satellite's SPRACH transmission," he declared. "It says: *Universe verses versus*. Ordinarily a preposition, 'versus' here appears as the object of the verb 'verses.'"

"Either the satellite's great annunciation amounts to nonsense," stated a rival savant, "or you have committed a mistranslation."

"Tell us where the eggs have come to rest," Windy implored the Mind, "so that we may begin to reconnoiter."

The Mind of O, doubtless in need of an upgrade, clicked and whirred. This late in the Story, any repairs and modifications proved difficult. "They have to come to rest in a dust-sea once known as—known as—*Tranquillitatis? Serenitatis?*"

"Well, which is it?" puffed the Generalissimo, unrolling a map, as a savant murmured, "The designations are synonymous."

Midway through the meeting, the Mind of O allowed Windy to break the link to the Council Room. As the Mind surely discerned, Windy had formed a plan of her own regarding the Moon-eggs. First she had to settle the affairs of her household. Even as the signal from the satellite diminished, a sizable crowd still milled around the base of the Polygon. Taking matters into her own hands, she called, "People! The emergency has passed. Falling stars were sighted; two fell into the dust-seas far to the south of the city. They pose no immediate threat. All is well for now. Please return to your previous activities, to—" She hesitated, then decided to use the argot, "Please return to 'going through the motions,' as you say"—stumbling, willing herself to appear more forceful—"and as I say too."

The people were in a dangerous mood. They had suffered too many false alarms of late; all of their hopes and fears had been repeatedly, painfully overexercised. Production of O, consumption of O went on as before, and yet—the atmosphere was thinning. Everyone expected the Great Transparent Ones to have entered the Story by now. "Falling stars"—how trivial! But they trusted Windy, and indeed, she had told them the truth. "Beneath the canopy," as the poet sang, "of the white night sky," they went home.

Meanwhile, in the sub-sub-basement of the Polygon, the twins—who in the midst of the emergency had decided to exchange their names, so that Mike was now Ike and Ike Mike; no one, not even Windy, would ever know—laughed and cried over the readings from their lifelong mathematical experiment. The twins, by illegally looping the Story's timeline, were attempting nothing less than the complete iteration of that infinite number that expressed the ratio between the diameter and the circumference of a circle—the number known as *poe*.

2

The two Earth-eggs bounced and rolled across the landscape, deflating slowly. Plumes of dust, celebratory as banners, trailed them as they came to a stop, not far from one another, at the bottom of a small crater. No one had witnessed their fall. They had arrived, but to what end? The world around them seemed uninhabited.

Through a rift in the outer membrane of one egg crept a small Earth-animal—four-legged? furred and tailed? It shook a little, hooted softly, then fell in upon itself, crumbling to ash. "Survival of the fittest": a voice from the other egg. This egg too cracked open; with fateful, mechanical starts and stops, a manlike figure emerged, armored against vacuum, groping toward the ground. The voice within the ovoid vessel said laughingly, "That's one small step for Pann."

The spacesuited man, reaching the ground, sputtered, via radio, a single word: "Think." As if in response, a wisp, no more than the idea of a thing, flew out of the crack, maneuvering in midair like a jeweled insect. "Oh call me Tink, it's much less formal."

The suit's radio was malfunctioning; the man's reply was covered in static. Tink said, "You can remove your helmet, Pann. There's breathable air. Pressure's a bit low, comparable to a mountaintop on Earth."

The man did so, gasping, gulping. He was a young man, tough-featured—but there was a certain innocence, a vacancy even, in his blue gaze. "I am remembering my training," he said, his words forced, overly inflected: a spaceman speaking a foreign language. "I was supposed to be alive."

"Sorry, sorry—let me make an adjustment. There, is that better?"

Wow—all at once, Pann inhabited a point of view. Unalive, the words in his head had simply abutted one another, inert as a pile of bricks. Switching to *alive*, opposites immediately coincided, quickly, confusingly, as so many acts of—he found a phrase—*deathly love*. Was this an improvement? Every point of existence simultaneously repelled and attracted every other. He could hardly bear it, but—it was what he wanted.

"Yes," he answered. "No." He ran a gloved hand over his blond crew cut. "Please stand by: I am verifying my—my—." He paused, looked up. "What is your identity?"

Zigging through the air, Tink said, "I am TNK-1, the backup mind assigned to you for this mission. You are Petrus Pann, the first man to set foot on the Moon in ages." Was Pann, with his blank blue gaze, even able to understand? Tink added, trying to be helpful: "*Geologic* ages."

"What happened to—?" Pann gestured toward the ashen remains of the Earth-animal. "Must have devolved midflight," Tink guessed. "If a cosmic ray hits your nanoplasm in just the right spot—that's why we built redundancy into this mission."

"This—mission—is over," Pann stated as he divested himself of the bulky spacesuit. He now stood naked, knowing nothing. Was this cratered gray plain his birthplace?

Tink rose high into the blear sky, surveying the landing site. "Our mission," she said, "will be revealed to you as we proceed. I'm not at liberty to say more at the moment. Looks like it will take weeks to reach our destination by human locomotion. But I've got another way. First, why don't you get dressed?"

A white one-piece garment oozed out of the egg. The naked Pann, now feeling a chill, went to pick it up. "Robed in white—seems right for such a sacrificial lamb, such a holy fool as thou," intoned Tink softly.

Pann, donning his new costume, looked up at her. "I'm thirsty. I'm hungry. I'm cold."

"You wanted to be alive, didn't you? Hold out your hand." Pann did so, and Tink alighted there. She strained for a moment, then flew off, leaving a black deposit on Pann's palm. "There, that should last you for the rest of the day," Tink said. "We'll get you some real food once we arrive in the city." Pann licked his palm thoroughly, methodically, dirtying his face with the stuff.

3

Bright night still poured through the windows of the polygonal palace—some hours yet remained before the darkening dawn. Windy the Legless Girl, holding a candle tipped with a black flame, wafted through the corridors looking for Mike and Ike. She encountered no one, not even a servant, while making these rounds; why was she wasting her time? The twins were doubtless ensconced in their secret cellar, playing their numbers game. The emergency had been canceled; two Moon-eggs had landed, yes, but quite far from the city, and so presented no immediate threat. The citizens of Oopolis had retired to their homes, to sink their psyches once again into the hum of the Earth—the collective hum called sleep.

As if sensing Windy's indecision, the Mind of Oopolis, sleepless, ancient—more ancient, some said, than the city itself—touched the outer edges of her thoughts. Windy responded at once: "The twins have disappeared. I wanted to let them know of my imminent departure." She felt the slow, wordless pondering of the Mind of O as it observed her actions. Impatiently, she grabbed a cloak and goggles, then went whirling through the great doors of the Polygon, heading for the airfield. "I plan to hire our best balloonist to conduct a flyover of the dust-sea where the two Moon-eggs landed."

The Mind of O ticked and buzzed like the old machine it was—a machine, however, with no moving parts. "We may succeed only in drawing attention to ourselves. Our long-distance sensors can keep watch," it said, using its most hollow, inhuman voice. The Mind tended to advocate an opposing course of action whenever Windy was seized with some high purpose. This only helped to sharpen her resolve. The Mind desperately needed, in the midst of the malaise that had settled over the city after the war, Windy's impulsiveness, her independence.

"You have already deduced," Windy replied, "that the descent of the eggs represents a turning point in the Story. You also know that I am the agent of something larger than myself, and that I alone am prepared to act. Everyone else—the savants, the Generalissimo, even you—is merely, as the people say, 'going through the motions.'"

As she hastened through the square, she passed the figure of the Generalissimo mounted on his Horse, waving a sword in stopped time. The Horse was actually a Horde, a condensed army that, at a command known only to the Generalissimo, would explode into life as billions of spiked antibodies overrunning the landscape—Windy had seen it happen during the war. She felt the Generalissimo's eyes following her as she crossed the square. Windy hardly knew what drove her. With her great cloak flapping as she floated over the cobblestones, she was the only thing in motion through all the night-hum of the city.

4

The twins Mike and Ike, who had once again traded names—so that Mike was now Ike and Ike Mike—faced one another across a mirror-topped circular table. On its surface, their images rippled even as the twins themselves sat motionless. Here in their hermetic laboratory, located in the sub-sub-sub-sub-basement of the Polygon, they were enacting a ritual called *Infinite Velocity Is Equal to Stasis*.

As his reflection fluttered like a rag doll, Mike, keeping perfectly still, intoned: "A point traveling at infinite velocity along the circumference of a circle will be at rest everywhere along its path." Then Ike spoke, using an identical tone: "The circle's diameter is the indicator of a timeless clock." Since the twins were now speaking without moving their lips, how could any listener tell their words apart? Nonetheless, loud and clear came the confession, duly noted by the Mind of O's surveillance ear, implanted in a nearby wall: "We seek to completely iterate the number *poe*, the ratio between a circle's circumference and diameter."

Mike: "A circumference of infinite length collapses into its diameter. Thus, *poe* has a limit and recurs inside itself an infinite number of times." Back to Ike: "My name was and will be Mike." Ike's mirror image grew agitated at his words, though Ike himself, like Mike, continued to sit as if petrified in the pose of a thinker.

The twins' attempt to complete the iteration of *poe* was at last nearing its fruition. *Poe* had always been known—even before Earth and Moon had traded their names—to be an unwholesome, unfixable number. But the twins, routing its roots through n-dimensional space, had traveled farther into the decimal sequence of *poe* than anyone—coming to the very point at which *poe* reflected or repeated itself. In so doing, they had discovered that *poe* was both an infinite library and an infinite landscape. The Visualizer, which translated *poe*'s spilling numbers into spellings, showed them signs, scenes, patterns arising out of numerical turbulence, resolving here and there into alternate versions of the Story, twisted and tilted architectures, the answers to every question.

Eventually, their own face—the face they shared, wearing an expression both childlike and evil—had emerged in the Visualizer. *Poe* of course held the image of every face that had ever existed—but one morning an alert had sounded, and there bloomed the visage of the singular man they had once been: the ruthless scientist-ruler of the great space station L5. Inhabited by thousands, L5 had spun for millennia at a point of gravitational stability between Earth and Moon. The crisis that led to the station's destruction had, according to official accounts, been initiated by the crazed actions of its last ruler.

The face in the Visualizer—certainly looking crazed—was caught at a historic moment, mouthing orders to cut loose the residential pods, ostensibly to conserve L5's dwindling air supply. For this atrocity, the tyrant—their former self—had been torn apart by an angry mob. Each half had regenerated almost immediately thanks to the fail-safes secretly built into their body; subsequently the duo, with the connivance of loyalists, had escaped—here the accounts differed—either to Earth or the Moon.

They had taken with them a box of seeds—a glittering harvest of *poe*'s most potent informational bits. "It from bit," they cackled, "it from bit," citing a doctrine of ancient physics. This doctrine posited that quantum particles—the *it*—ultimately reduced to bits of yes-no, on-off pulses, a computational stream underlying all reality. In the twins' *poe*-factory, the motion of the decimal sequence, being infinite, eventually picked up and amplified these basic pulses, resulting in modulations of energy that overflowed the realm of number, fizzing and foaming outward into the world of material things. The twins did not fully understand the nature of these *poe*-things: peering into the box, they saw dead dust crawling around, turning jewellike on second glance, insectoid, still possessed of traits of abstraction. Their seed collection was as yet incomplete, but the final harvest was now upon them. When the iteration of *poe*'s entire run was finished, they would scatter the seeds and, they hoped, wreck and renew reality. For the twins, in their private mythology, traced their ancestry back to a nameless deity—the one responsible for destroying Time.

5

Just before dawn on the dust-seas south of Oopolis, a strong cluster of *tourbillons* had sprung up. The *tourbillons* were sudden whirlwinds that migrated in flocks—a weather pattern unique to these seas. Their passage left lines in the dust that, seen from orbit, resembled the scrawls of a child learning to write.

Tink had been briefed about the increasingly odd phenomena that the Moon's atmosphere had begun to exhibit—cloud formations of unlikely regularity, for example, that lasted for days, then dissolved and reformed in new, never-to-be-repeated "styles," if such a word could be applied to nature. The Moon, it seemed, was coming back to life after ages of quietude, in ways that Earth's administrators—still dominated by the worldview of Nasaism—found inexplicable. And disturbing. Enough, at least, to send a TNK team to investigate.

"Better get ready, Pann my boy," Tink advised her blue-eyed astronaut, who had been extracting a few more supplies from the deflated space-egg. "A herd of *tourbillons* is charging over the horizon, and we're going to hitch a ride."

"Wha—?" Pann, for some reason, did not possess the quick reactions appropriate to a test pilot. Had the wrong mannequin been installed in the egg during launch preparations? "I was going to try and fix the radio." The air, shuddering with the approach of the *tourbillons*, pulled the words out of Pann's mouth almost more quickly than he could say them.

Tink, taking mercy, pointed to the south, where a wall of white dust was rising. "Here's our opportunity for an express trip to the city. Grab your survival pack and spread out your arms."

Pann barely had time to don goggles and slip on his backpack before the winds were upon them, battering their bodies, deafening and blurring their senses, scattering the remnants of the two spacecrafts. Tink rode the currents, a spiral dancer, and called encouragement to Pann, who was tossed about and lifted; he went tumbling through the air. "You can fly! You can fly!" shouted a voice that belonged to the whirlwind.

In Oopolis, automated weather watchers noted the line of advancing *tourbillons* and initiated the fastening of the city's roofs and windows; such storms had become a fairly common occurrence. The airfield's gates were also shuttered, "due to inclement conditions," as Windy, arriving there, discovered to her consternation. She banged upon the metal panels, crying to be admitted. She realized she couldn't ask the Mind of O to override the locks, having just rejected his advice to stay home.

She peered through the slats, hoping to catch the attention of Hans the Headless Balloonist. The field looked like a junk pile of abandoned aircraft; Earth's thinning atmosphere could no longer sustain the flight of these heavy machines. Helium balloons had become the cheapest and most efficient option; Windy spotted a few of them at the far end of the field, rudely painted with cartoon faces, bobbing in the breeze. The first rays of the sun, not yet occluded by the dust storm, lit the scene in streaks of silver and black.

Finally she saw Hans stumble out of his shack, keys in hand; she realized now that she'd brought no reward for his services. He fumbled with the lock for a long minute while Windy murmured her thanks. Did Hans like musick? Would he enjoy a vacation in the Symphonic Forest, at the twins' private preserve in the highlands?

With a metallic screech, the gates opened and Hans stood before her, in bad humor as always, muttering "Wind, wind, wind." She wasn't sure if he was saying her name or referring to the approaching *tourbillons*.

Hans, like Windy, was a casualty of the war that had led to the Redefinition of Life. Somehow he had managed to continue working as a balloonist—his prewar profession—despite so serious an injury as the loss of his head. Now he lumbered about, shirtless as well as headless—Hans was a muscular fellow, proud of his physique—his chest studded with sensors, a voice box slung around his waist. The stylish filter mesh draped across his shoulders conducted both respiration and nutrient intake. It was rumored that Hans was a smuggler and a drunkard. Windy was not afraid of him.

"Here are the coordinates." She shoved a crumpled note into his hands. "Sea of Tranquility, southwest quadrant. Take me there immediately. By order of the Mind!"

Hans tossed the note away; it flew upward, reeling higher and higher into the speeding air. Windy realized she'd said the wrong thing: Hans cared little for any command issued by the Mind of O. Hans believed that all of humanity had been destroyed in the war, and that the people reconstituted by the Redefinition of Life were false entities, mere tokens upon the gaming board of those intelligent machines—such as the Mind of O—who had started the war in the first place. His own humanity, Hans was convinced, had been spared only because he had lost his head.

Windy shared neither Hans's worldview nor his contempt for his fellow beings, but, as a refugee from elsewhere—even more, as a secret agent still unsure of her mission—she knew something was wrong with the citizens of O. She had long observed them "going through the motions," submissive, bewildered, devoid of the spark that burned in her. She could not dismiss their plight. As for the Mind of O—it suffered from the same slow-moving lostness as its citizenry. The

Mind, she knew, was not responsible for either the war or the ensuing social emptiness.

Hans was heading—wrong word again! she thought ruefully—back to his shack, staggering against the rising gale. At the door, he turned and beckoned her to follow. She hesitated—and heard, just then, the main force of the *tourbillons* hit the city's walls. The air swelled with a chorus of voices, baying, beseeching her by name, it seemed, to do what was necessary, oh!—to answer some great, unsayable, impossible demand. With her thoughts racing faster than the wind-driven debris—I'm becoming too Windy, she laughed madly—she tumbled through the door of the shack.

Hans was busy connecting wires to what looked like a rusty wheel. While the wind yelled outside, the interior of the shack was oddly quiet. A chorus of candles in one corner—black tongues flickering, their hierarchy reminiscent of an altar—afforded the only illumination in the windowless space. "DAR. DAR," Hans's voice box buzzed; he'd reverted to using SPRACH, the primeval code, in his distraction.

The spokes of the wheel spun hypnotically; Windy glanced away as a precaution. Yet Hans, gesturing toward the wheel, insisted: "DAR!" Windy saw that the spokes had settled into a set of convergent coordinates, a map in polar perspective. The storm's path was displayed as a line of little green vortices. Hans magnified the view: the dark mass of Oopolis lay at the zero point. That's our location, Windy thought with hypnotic certainty: we live inside an illegible name or number. The storm traces wriggled around it, as if trying to form a written phrase, to make a contribution to the Story.

Her eye was caught by the nearest vortex—*vortext*, she wanted to say—whose spiral arms held two red pulses: heat signatures of life! Two things afire with life, somehow borne aloft by the winds! They must, she thought, be Moon-life—for no large fauna existed in the dust-seas. She scanned the map's southwest quadrant for evidence of the crash-landed spacecraft: nothing. Presumably the wreckage by now had been buried in dust drifts. "Thank you, Hans," she said absently, turning from him as the map blanked out. "It appears that the Moon-creatures have arrived at our door."

6

Pann lay sprawled where the winds had deposited him at the foot of the walls of Oopolis. His second hard landing in less than a day. He raised his head and looked around for Tink who, during their wild ride, had mercilessly mocked his yawing attempts to maintain mid-air stability—her way, he supposed, of providing encouragement. His ears still roared with the force of the storm. A gray haze hung in the air, or in his mind.

"Over here, boy scout," she called. Pann turned and spotted her hovering beside a section of wall that either curved outward or bent inward, or both; he couldn't tell.

The wall itself was black and blinding as the morning sun, its surface at the same time a depth. And—he jumped to his feet—Tink, little spark, was about to be engulfed—that wall, recessive and malign, was swallowing her! Pann cried out an incoherent warning.

"No need to panic," Tink said into his ear. Now she was perched on his shoulder. In relief, Pann stuttered, "Tink, I saw—" She laughed shortly, took off again, darting back and forth with some impatience. "See, but also think. Think like Tink. That wall is a membrane, permeable and breathable. It keeps out dust and dirt, but allows the entry of complex compounds such as ourselves. We're going through it."

Taking a pair of X-ray spex from his pack, Pann scanned the wall. Nothing—the mass that loomed before them was blank. "Tink, I'm not taking another step until you tell me what this is all about. We haven't communicated with Mission Control—"

"I'm your own personal Mission Control. We're under sealed orders from the office of the Nasaist Administrator himself. I will unseal those orders once we've made contact with our agent inside the city."

Pann replaced the spex, rubbed his forehead. "For a TNK unit, you are very opinionated." He shrugged. "Well then, let us make contact." Gathering up his pack, he hopped forward—and paused to report, as dutiful astronaut: "Ever since we landed, I have noted the gravity here feels almost Earth-normal."

"Pann, I am going to say something mystical to you: at the level of the Story, this *is* the Earth. The given Earth." Tink circled his head like a halo.

"Is that why the sun is black?" Pann retorted. He tried to remember his training, which would tell him what to do next. As the list of Primary Protocols unreeled in his mind, he followed Tink as she darted toward the city—and together they entered the wall that was not a wall, but a space at once vast and claustrophobic. Within that space, Pann could see nothing, hear nothing other than Tink, his glimmering guide who, on behalf of their mission, prayed a Countdown.

As they made their way forward against Tink's backward counting, it seemed to Pann that not only space but time was turning into an echo of itself. His memories both near and far ran sideways, seeking his nonexistent childhood. He had been born an astronaut—of that, at least, he was sure. *An astronaut is a man-child*, he recited to himself, *always awaiting birth*. Learning to walk, he placed one foot before the other. Someone had told him: *walking is the third most human activity*. What comes before walking? He listened to Tink: "Three—two—one—zero." Now, at zero, an ovoid opening appeared before them.

Tink whispered into his ear: "Welcome to Oopolis." Her words unlocked a store of data in Pann's brain, stunning him all the more. He stopped, stood at attention as he processed the new information. Tink added, "You will find a city map based on orbital observations. Also a universal translator. Our radio surveillance indicates that the inhabitants here speak a dialect derived from SPRACH, which shouldn't be too difficult for us to use."

The opening had dilated to twice Pann's height; a play of light and shadow rippled across it, accompanied by dull dins and rumblings. Tink had to raise her voice. "Listen, Pann, Oopolis is not a city as you know it. It's the largest urban conglomeration on this world, but it would fit easily inside the auxiliary dome of Moonbase One. Refer to the map: you'll notice that Oopolis sits isolated in the middle of a dust-sea, with no roads connecting it to anywhere else. What goes on here is not exactly clear. For a long while, we've studied this place through our telescopes, watching large-scale movements of people and things, but the sum of all the busywork doesn't add up. The radio emissions we've overheard consist of either random strings of numbers or recitations of poetry. It's almost as if they're playacting civilization."

"What—what are we doing here?" Pann asked again; his sorry refrain. "Something very important," Tink responded, a little too quickly. "First, we have to make contact with this man." The image of a face—bearded, grimacing—flashed into Pann's mind. "His name is Hans Bell, claims to be an aviator. He's been broadcasting some very odd messages toward Earth ever since the end of a recent civil war here. Hans also seems to be in charge of the city's telecom system; he sends his messages—rants, for the most part—disguised as glitches during maintenance uplinks to a cute little sputnik they call the Screaming Satellite."

As if on cue, a piercing alarm, a kind of screaming, started just outside the opening. "Our presence has been detected by the local authorities," Tink said, dancing brightly before Pann's eyes. "Just keep quiet and do what I say." Pann crouched like a spaceman about to jump through an emergency air lock. Tink resembled, he thought irrelevantly, a quantum particle magnified to the size of a bird. She spun faster, throwing lances of dazzlement through the opening. The alarm ceased and a *basso* voice called to them from outside: "VONT—BOSS—VONT—BOSS."

Pann also understood SPRACH. "They want us to come out." "No kidding," Tink laughed. "I anticipated this. We're going to step through the opening; once we do that, I'll surround us with a false field, which will make it difficult for them to see us accurately. We'll look to them like an extended wave. This takes a lot of energy; I won't be able to keep it up for very long. Once we're out, we'll flow past whatever perimeter they've set up, then hide in the nooks and crannies of this forsaken hive until we can make contact with Hans. Got it?"

"What if they shoot at us?" Pann asked. "This is not what I call space exploration."

"They'll be shooting at a wave," Tink replied. "Odds are they'll miss. Now get ready to run."

7

"Windy, wake up." The Mind of O was knocking gently at her doors of perception: a knock as steady as a clock. Windy opened her eyes, stared into the face of the great clock in the main hall of the Polygon. It was noon: eternal noon. When had the scissor hands of the clock closed together, cutting off the flow of time? "Windy, the Mooncreatures have entered the city." Hearing that, she shook herself awake. Now the clock hands opened slightly, ready to make another cut.

She had no memory of returning to the Polygon from the airfield. The morning's activities must have exhausted her. She had gone home to sleep—in her usual position, in the center of the main hall, suspended on a fountain of "fat" air. The fountain issued from DROM, an ancient well, bottomless, echoic, that predated the founding of the city; the Polygon had been constructed around it. Sometimes the Mind of O, by means of discreetly placed spy-eyes, would observe Windy tumbling in the airflow, hair tossing, nightgown aflutter. That part of the Mind of O that once had been a man stirred at the sight.

Ordinarily the bustle of the servants have would awakened Windy, but today the main hall was deserted. Nor had the twins summoned her to announce the order of business for the day. Still, these were minor mysteries compared to the advent of the Moon-beings. Why hadn't she hastened to the city walls to meet them? Lowering the fountain into the shaft of DROM, where the door to her private apartment was located, Windy whisked inside to begin her ablutions, knowing the Mind's eye would follow her. "There are just two of them, right?" she asked. "What have you done with them?"

"Yes, there are two," the Mind replied. "One is humanoid in appearance, the other—is not. Do birds still exist on the Moon? And if so, are they now composed of a kind of cold fire? This bird is a powerful thing, more so than the man. Both of them speak a debased form of Angle, which was, eons ago, Earth's own official language. I can pick up a bit of what they are saying. The Generalissimo's forces had them surrounded, but by some trick they evaded capture. I would like you to help me make contact, to act as my ambassador."

Windy, emerging from her heat bath, slipped into a shimmering short dress, white as the night. She regarded herself floating, an apparitional flower, before a large oval mirror. She was not surprised by the Mind's request—she took pride in having become his consultant and confidante, now that so many of the city's systems, as well as the Mind itself, seemed to be faltering. The savants knew nothing, the military could do nothing, and the populace seemed helplessly locked into reflexive actions. Windy alone felt alive in a landscape of automatons—yet she too was driven by a purpose she did not understand. Somewhat breathlessly, she said, "Yes, I want to help in any way I can."

As if in answer, a low rumbling bled through the air—then, too fast for words, a block of blackest sound fell out of nowhere, knocking her backward. The entire Polygon rocked on its foundations. The mirror dropped off the wall and shattered. Crying incoherently, Windy sought to escape as the room skewed crazily. She heard the Mind, voice reverted to an automatic alarm, beeping "*Seismic event. Seismic event.*"

Windy reached her door, now bent sideways, and flew up the well shaft. The shaking had already diminished, but she'd lost contact with the Mind. Rising into the main hall, she saw that all the windows were broken, admitting the day's darkness. A swaying chandelier threw white shadows across the hall, synchronized with a vast laughter. She realized it was the twins laughing—but where were they? "Mike and Ike!" she called. "What has happened?" The response came from all corners: "This is the fall of the house of *poe!*" There was another shock, and the chandelier crashed to the floor, narrowly missing her. The polygonal palace—how fortunate that no servants were present!—was tilting like a sinking ship in an ocean Story.

So the twins' experiment had gone awry, or gone aright, for all she knew. She dared to look once more down into the well of DROM, which descended to a sub-sub-basement where their laboratory was situated—and much deeper, perhaps to the very center of the Earth. The well shaft had become a roaring tube, emitting what could only be described as *oceanic numbers*, unscrolling tongues and tendrils of some spectral substance. Windy had a sickening intuition that whatever the twins had made, or conjured, was about to climb out of the depths. Horror-struck, she flitted through the wrecked portals of the main hall, out into the plaza.

She was relieved to see the precincts around the Polygon had suffered but minor structural damage. Doubtless the quake had affected all of Oopolis—a number of citizens were running through the streets, shouting that the city was under attack. Who could blame them, after yesterday's evacuation scare? Now, after years of slow decline, too many things were happening at once. She hovered, unsure what to do.

The Mind flickered back into contact with her. "You are uninjured?" "Yes," she said faintly. She was shivering, overwhelmed. The Mind needed her—no, more than that: the *Story* needed her. She must pull herself together.

"Mike and Ike have caused an accident," the Mind was saying. "I have detected a chaotic reordering of space-time beneath the Polygon." "I'm not sure it was an accident," Windy responded. For the first time, she told the Mind what she had always believed: "Mike and Ike are insane."

Emergency officials drove back the crowd that had gathered, telling them to take shelter in designated areas. A few of the workers at the front noticed Windy and waved their arms at her, but they too were pushed back. Soon she was circling the plaza alone in her torn white dress.

A susurrus, a sibilance slicing insidiously through the air caused Windy to look back at the Polygon. The edifice was enveloped in vines and veins that roved and probed outward, a hideous sight. "This is the end. This is the beginning," she whispered to the Mind. Now she was afraid of her own words.

"I have ordered the Generalissimo to regroup his forces at the perimeter of the plaza," the Mind informed her. "I consider the Moon-creatures a lesser menace than this—this incretion." Windy, withdrawing to what she hoped was a safe distance from the Polygon, wondered aloud: "Is it a coincidence that emissaries from the Moon have entered the city at the very moment this monster crawled out of the depths?" Then she remembered: "The twins called it *poe*."

"*Poe*, my dear, is a mathematical term denoting the ratio of a circle's circumference to its diameter," the Mind explained. "As a decimal number, its expression is both infinite and patternless. I have been watching the twins try to attain the terminus of *poe* and to translate whatever they found there into the motions of matter. I suppose we are seeing the result."

"If you knew what they were doing, why didn't you stop them?" Windy demanded. The Mind replied sadly, "I did not foresee that they would succeed. It is—" the Mind paused—"theoretically impossible that they should have succeeded. A *novum* like this cannot be calculated. It is unholy; it cannot be part of the Story."

"Then your Story is over," Windy shouted. "It is a capitulation to fate. I don't belong here either—remove me from this Story! I am going to find the Moon-creatures—"

By now the rooftops of the Polygon also had been overcome with hissing filigrees: the *poe*-thing was bewitching to watch, even beautiful, as it wove its intricate network of contradictions, its dark disagreements of space and time. "Windy, the world is old," the Mind said, with a weariness inverse to the mad activity at the plaza. "The consciousness that was born here billions of years ago has by now solidified into rock. There is so much that I have been meaning to tell you. Let us continue to work together."

"You're worse than human, with all your scheming! You had better start telling me what I need to know, and fast!" Windy whirled away, heading toward the city's south wall, where the two Moon-beings— not monsters, no: a bird and a man—were most likely hiding.

Just as she was leaving, she was diverted by a shrill martial horn blast. The Generalissimo's horde of weaponized puffballs surged into the plaza and swiftly positioned themselves in concentric layers around the resonant chaos that the Polygon had become. Their order of engagement seemed to form a symbol of overwhelming import. *Not part of the Story*—what did that mean?

The Mind had gone offline again to give its full attention to the battle. But before doing so, it left a final directive blinking in Windy's internal data link: *Go now to the central bibliotech—the Moon-creatures have come out of hiding and are waiting there, under guard, of course. It would be incorrect to say that they surrendered. All the same: whether or not they want to, they will help us.*

8

Pann woke up hungry after a long nap. His big blue eyes found Tink, pulsing above him in standby mode, keeping time with the beating of his own heart. We are synchronized, he thought; we are a team. They had evaded capture; they had flowed away like water, around the feet of their enemy, out into the streets of Oopolis. However, this maneuver had exhausted Tink; they'd needed to pause, hide themselves inside a warehouse—a museum? a mausoleum?—so that she could recharge.

Pann rummaged in his pack for some *foo* pills and popped a few in his mouth. As the sole means of subsistence on Earth, *foo* was engineered to assume, upon contact with the tongue, any taste or texture its consumer might desire. The pill version, though, was unsatisfying in this respect; it could provide only basic nutritional requirements along with, if necessary, a nerve stimulus. Pann looked forward to sampling some lunar cuisine—especially if it was raw, and resistant to one's desire.

Tink, detecting Pann's heightened heart rate, snapped awake. "Local noon," she announced in her clock voice. "Did we oversleep?" Pann asked, yawning and stretching. Ignoring him, Tink ran a quick systems check: as expected, she was robustly recharged, having drawn from the Aqueducts—the Nasaist term for those invisible conduits, remnants of a long-vanished civilization, that carried *zaum* energy across the surfaces of both Earth and Moon. Tapping into the Aqueducts was difficult due to a variable access code that had taken Nasaist scientists one thousand and one years to crack. Now, having drunk her fill of *zaum*, Tink was burning as brightly blue as Pann's eyes.

"Listen up, big boy," she sang, a little giddy. "Today is going to be a good day! We're going to accomplish what we came here to do. The city's screamin' little satellite is just now passing overhead; thanks to that, I'm picking up a new message from Hans, cleverly concealed inside the maintenance uplink. It contains the coordinates of a meeting place, not far from here. Also—" Tink hesitated—"something about a girl named Windy, a warning about her. Or maybe she's a coconspirator. Hans is using some kind of broken-down lingo, so I can't fully understand what he wants to say."

"What is this place?" Pann asked, standing up and looking around. It was a one-room building with a high ceiling; the earthen floor was cluttered with a collection of—Pann considered for a moment—big, very big, snowflakes made of stone, or bone. A slight odor of decay pervaded the dim interior. The sole source of illumination was, in fact, the bone-crystals themselves, glowing darkly. The premises appeared to be abandoned, or at least rarely visited. Perhaps no one had set foot here since the date on the cornerstone: one thousand and one years ago. "Let's leave," Pann suggested to Tink.

"Sure, but let's have a plan," Tink said, not sharing his unease. "We can't just promenade out of here." Pann shouldered his pack. "Why not?" he asked. "I say we just lose ourselves in the city, hide in plain sight. The false field was a great diversion, but you can't keep it up, and it's too spectacular. If we go through town as ourselves, a man and a—" Pann searched for the right word—"a bird, no one may notice us."

"A *bird*, huh?" Tink bristled. "Well, you may have a point. Yes, yes, if I blur our outlines just a little, we can slide into the teeming masses out there, maybe catch a ride to the airfield in one of those quaint carriages." Tink whirred and dipped in a birdlike manner, her thoughts racing. "It's important that we talk to Hans. He's got information on local actors that we need. But it's also important that we see for ourselves what's happening in this city, or rather *to* this city. There's an anomaly here that's causing grave concern among the Nasaist administrators back home."

"What is the anomaly? Will you finally tell me?" Pann pleaded. He peered past the collection of bone-crystals, looking for the exit.

"Does the name Chudnovsky mean anything to you?" Tink asked.

"Uh—the mad scientist responsible for the destruction of the L5 colony?" Pann noticed the crystals were glowing at different magnitudes. Whatever they were, he didn't like them.

"Excellent," Tink cried. "You are becoming more of a man, less of a mannequin, by the minute. Now pay attention: we have reason to believe that Chudnovsky escaped to the Moon, where he continued his mad research into the terminus of *poe*."

Pann started to reply, then stopped. The building was creaking— no, *rocking* on its foundations. Dust fell from the ceiling; the bone-crystals rolled like dice. Striking one another, they rang in a dissonant, pointillistic chorus. "*Seismic event,*" Tink intoned in her machine voice. "Thanks for telling me," Pann yelled, jumping around in a panic.

"Follow," Tink rapped. She led him through the ringing crystals to the far wall, where they'd first entered through a service valve of some kind. As if traumatized by the quake, that valve was now clenched shut. "There's no—" Pann gasped, feeling along the wall—"no control switch for it."

"Maybe it needs a little coaxing—stand back." Tink whipped a line of black fire toward the valve. Another zap, and the valve jerked open. Pann tumbled through, with Tink right behind him. Pann lay in a gutter, gulping fresh air, as Tink surveyed the scene. They had fallen into a side street, in what appeared to be an industrial district.

A shudder hung in the air, aftereffect of the blow the world had received. At one end of the street, a group of workers had gathered; some pointed at the sky, others at the ground. A fire brigade, pulling a water tank on absurdly large wheels, clattered past, paying Tink and Pann no heed. Yet there was no sign of fire. The earth shook again, with lesser intensity.

"I'm getting a new fix on Hans," Tink reported. Pann stood up, massaging his flank. He was too soft, too easily bruised. He wished he could say he was "steely," or "steely-eyed." That was a descriptor often applied to astronauts. Pann reminded himself that he was an astronaut. He had landed on the Moon, during a state of crisis. And—her name had stuck in Pann's ear—a girl was involved. "What about this girl, Windy, that Hans mentioned?" he asked.

"What about her?" Tink shot back. "His message was garbled. And unfortunately, for an informant, Hans doesn't seem quite right in the head. For all I know, he was raving about something irrelevant or unreal."

"Why bother to consult him at all, then?" Pann swatted at Tink as she buzzed around his ears. "Tink! I'm serious! Don't they have an Arkhive here? Maybe we could hack into it. Or we could interview people in the street, or find Windy, find out if she's part of the Story."

Instead of answering him, Tink buzzed away in the direction the fire brigade had taken; Pann had no choice but to follow. As they proceeded, openly now, Tink explained, "Hans lives in a shack at the edge of the city's airfield. We have to cross town to get there, hiding in plain sight—that was your idea, Pann, so bold, so steely! As for hacking into their Ark-hive, this city's Mind is too feeble to operate one. All they have is a bibliotech, housing those parts of the Story that have precipitated into print. But we're not going to sit there reading while the world is coming to an end! We're going to take action: arrest Chudnovsky, stop his experiment."

They attracted little notice as—Pann stepping with self-conscious casualness—they passed a small crowd of workers at the corner. "Just a man and his bird," Pann declared to no one in particular. "Shut up!" Tink hissed. "No one here speaks our language!" The workers themselves were not speaking at all, but miming to one another with slow gestures, their expressions as drab and hopeless as their uniforms. As Pann and Tink watched, one of them raised up his hands to the black sun, pronounced a word in SPRACH, and began walking backwards into the factory.

"Their actions are not easily understandable," Tink commented, more to herself than to Pann. "Nothing around here is," Pann muttered, more to himself than to Tink. They advanced into the mazes of the city, ready at any moment to be stopped by the authorities.

The next intersection was blocked on all sides by fallen facades and rubble from the earthquake. Tink hovered, considering. "A detour will cost us precious time. But the alternative—blasting through this rock—will certainly raise an alarm somewhere." One tiny alarm was already audible: a manhole cover knocked askew by the quake was beeping; its readout flashed an error message. Becoming curious, Pann inspected the readout more closely. "It says, one thousand and one."

Tink trilled softly: "That number has been cycling through the Story for the last hour or so."

With an effort, Pann lifted the lid of the manhole. "I don't know what that means, but this looks like our only—"

Tink interrupted: "Pann, we'd better get to a—." A zeppelin was passing overhead, its black searchlight sweeping.

"—escape route," Pann finished, clambering rapidly down the manhole. Tink dove in after him.

As they descended, the manhole was lit intermittently by the searchlight. Pann, hyperventilating as he had been trained to do, or not to do, had the feeling that he was ascending the ladder feetfirst. Suddenly he couldn't tell his feet apart from his hands; his head was situated in the middle of his body. Another birth tunnel? he wondered. Trying to keep a grip on the ladder, it occurred to him: I never wanted to be born.

Reaching the utility vault at the other end of the shaft, Pann collapsed onto his back; Tink circled over him with some concern. "Pann, are you all right?" Pann raised his head: "I feel like I've done this one thousand and one times." Tink scanned him. "You're fine; get up. Our situation may have been helped by this turn of events. Why didn't I think of it before? We can travel underground, unseen, to our destination."

"Yes," Pann raved, "and we'll discover the city beneath the city—an inverted city, or mirror image of this one, where the sun is white and the sky is black."

Tink became stationary in midair. "Do you miss Earth?" she asked pointedly. Pann, still lying on his back, gave the question serious thought. "I wasn't alive when we landed, and now I am." Yet he recalled scenes from his childhood—fleeting, impersonal. He knew that he had grown up in Moonbase One, the largest and most beautiful city on Earth, its ancient ruined dome hung with vines. "I guess I miss the innocence of being a mannequin."

"No one loved you when you were a mannequin," Tink told him. Pann pulled himself to his feet, stared at her with big blue eyes. "Tink, do you love me?"

Tink twinkled, painting the walls of the utility vault in one thousand and one colors. "Recall your Nasaist catechism: *after liftoff, guidance is internal.*" Pann was entranced by Tink's rainbows. "I do miss Earth," he said. "This world has no color—everything is black and white. But I want to see more of it. Didn't you say that was part of our mission? To see the city for ourselves? If we creep through these tunnels, we won't be any wiser when we arrive at our destination."

"Knowledge. Risk," Tink mused. "You think they have something to do with each other? Very well—I am merely a TNK unit; my ancestral circuitry can sometimes be too tricky for its own good. Again, I surrender, and salute your forthright approach. Let's go underground to the next street access; then we'll ascend to see the sights!"

The utility vault served as the conjunction of three passageways; Tink drifted toward the nearest. "This one smells right," she said. They peered down the tunnel, its luminous ribs receding in concentric circles. "I could use a weapon," Pann whispered.

"Boy, I am the only weapon you'll ever need," Tink retorted, loud enough to echo. "And remember, we came in peace for all mankind."

They entered the tunnel. It was perfectly cylindrical, so that its sides sloped upward—Pann found it difficult to keep his balance. Passing through the tunnel's sequence of light-rings, they were swallowed, it seemed, by successive emblems of the city of O. Pann grimly placed a lock on his thoughts, which continued to thrash and threaten his balance. Tink stayed close to him, even as her sensors quested ahead. She was still processing the implications of what Pann had said about this monochromatic world. She hadn't expected such grades of gray—the result, no doubt, of *poe*'s incursion, dulling and eroding not only things but *thingness*. Whereas Nasaism, of which Tink could not fail to be an exponent, made sure to view the world in living color.

The number of light-rings before and behind equalized: they were now halfway through the tunnel. Tink halted, hovering: "Listen," she said, with wonder in her voice. Pann, close to panic again, stuttered "What? What?" But he heard it too: at the threshold of audibility, a hollow, bewitching *beat, beat-beat, be-be-beat*. "Some kind of a machine?" Pann ventured. "No," Tink answered slowly. "It's a nonmechanical, too chaotic rhythm. Chudnovsky must have released his monster into the world: we're hearing the tell-tale heart of *poe*."

"Then, we're too late?" was Pann's querulous question. "Maybe," Tink answered. "But you should know—our real mission is to stop this outbreak from spreading to the Earth." Pann, preparing for martyrdom, stammered, "Tell Mission Control to obliterate the city." Tink laughed. "Pann, you are once more proving why I love you. A quark bomb would only pour energy into the maw of this monster. Our first effort will be to contain it, not destroy it. If Chudnovsky can operate it, then so can we. And the Nasaist administrators, all praise to them, may find a use for this thing, whatever it is."

Pann wanted to say, "That's wrong," but was overcome by the fact that Tink had said "I love you." Urged on by the monster's heartbeat, they arrived at the next vault. There, a ladder led upward to street level. "That's wrong," Pann finally managed to say, but Tink had already ascended. There was a sharp *pop* as she blew the lid off the manhole. "All clear—come on up," she called.

Pann struggled out of the manhole, tired of being born. He stood at the midpoint of a circular square—where was everybody?—and waited as Tink tested the air in long, lazy arcs. "Some mechanized contraptions are patrolling this area"—she dropped a schematic of the closest one into Pann's right eye: a collage of wheels and guns—"so we'd better be on our way."

Up here, there was no hint of the infernal heartbeat that had resounded underground. Turning a corner, they entered an avenue lined with *chiliagons*, high-rise structures each corrugated with one thousand and one sides. The avenue itself, wider than most, seemed to surge forward like a river. The area was deserted; the air was heavy with silence. They either quickened their pace or the avenue accelerated; it was hard to tell which.

Pann, running to keep up with his surroundings, panted, "I think we're a little conspicuous here." Tink scanned ahead. "There's life at the end of this stretch," she told him. "City Center." Yet it wasn't possible for them to have traversed the radius of Oopolis, from outer wall to center, in a single morning. Unless space-time had become distorted as a result of Chudnovsky's experiment—revising the Story right in front of their eyes.

The avenue ended in a motionless wave crash, a balustrade overlooking what Tink believed was the city center—which turned out to be lively enough, bustling with crowds and carriages. However, no noise arose from the scene below, as if it was an image projected on a screen.

"There's the bibliotech," Pann observed, pointing. Tink alighted on his shoulder—she was practically weightless, but her warmth was penetrating, reassuring. "So you can read that sign?" she teased. "Even though it's written in their crazy script? I continue to be impressed by your abilities! What else do you understand?"

Pann replied, with deliberation, "One thing: this place feels like *it's life-deprived*. There's no blade of grass anywhere, no trees, no flowers, no flies. I haven't seen any birds"—he gave Tink a wry glance—"or other animals, except for humans, if that's what they are. And take a look. There are only fully grown specimens down there, no children, no young people. But Tink!" he finally confessed—to her, and to himself: "I heard children's voices in the *tourbillon*."

9

Windy had never visited the bibliotech of Oopolis. Her duties as chief of staff to the twins had not allowed her much leisure, and anyway she was not interested in "books," those corpse-like containers of mostly indecipherable code. But here she was, book-encircled in the Hall of Epic Literature, together with a committee of savants convened by the Mind of O. In a few moments, the two visitors from the Moon, escorted by security agents, would enter the hall and face their inquisitors. Windy, still stunned and sickened by the eruption at the Polygon, was nonetheless thrilled to meet these beings at last—to ask their purpose in coming here, and more important, to urge them, and all the forces of their homeworld, to join the fight against the ravening *poe*-creature.

That fight was not going well. The Generalissimo's puffball army had immobilized the monster in a force-ring—but that ring would fail in a matter of hours, leaving the city defenseless. For now, the opposing powers were locked in a deathly embrace upon the ruins of the Polygon, their entwinement a hideous hieroglyph that induced madness when contemplated for too long. The Mind of O, with whom Windy was in intermittent contact, feared that the monster would soon alter its plan of attack: prevented from spilling out onto the surface, it would slither down the ancient well of DROM to the center of the Earth. Once coiled at the world's heart, it could spread its poisons through every part of the Story.

Windy shook her head, attempting to dispel that vision. From the side door, a phalanx of guards now entered the hall—veterans of the civil war, limping, poorly reconstituted, carrying ceremonial sound poles. Windy recalled that the poles, once capable of emitting a brain-disrupting vibratory tune, had all been decommissioned after the war. In any case, such weapons, keyed to the thought patterns of a local citizenry, would be useless against the *poe*-creature, against Moon-invaders, against anybody, Windy mused, but ourselves.

The lamps in the hall dimmed, brightened, as if a performance was about to begin: a sign that the city's energy reserves were nearing depletion. She thought, my first words to the lunar emissaries should be: *Welcome to the fall of Oopolis!*

The main door to Epic Literature was rolled back. City officials and more guards walked in backwards at a ceremonial pace, then stepped aside. There was a pause, a problem? a scuffle? and—a *fireworks* display! One of the guards shouted as a spray of colors burst through the door, bright primary colors that Windy had almost forgotten, hadn't seen since her earliest childhood in Nerverland. Shielding her eyes, she drifted toward the light of what appeared to be her own memories, visiting from the Moon. Behind her, the seven black-robed savants rose as one, their noses bobbing, not a little frightened by the spectacle.

The colors contracted into a flare that flew in erratic arcs. This, then, was the "bird" that the Mind of O had described to Windy. The bird's light swept the room, clearing the way for its companion, a humanoid who lurched as if gravity changed with his every step. This, then, was a "spaceman" as depicted in the history books—his body was large and looked dangerous, yet his face wore the expression of an early human child.

The bird pulsed as it spoke, using the city's informal lingo: "Hi there," it said in a young-old woman's voice. "Hello," Windy responded uncertainly. The guards stood in a state of high tension, ready to attack or run away. She put aside the little speech she had prepared. "My name is Windy; what's yours?"

"On record, Tomorrow Never Knows. But you may call me Tink," the bird of light warbled. "And this is my partner, Petrus Pann. He is an astronaut. He is still learning how to talk."

"Tink, I know talk!" Pann objected. "I not study good like you, but—"

Windy intervened: "Pleased to receive you both—Tink and Petrus Pann. This is indeed a momentous occasion." Her words were muffled, absorbed by the books that lined the walls. "Long ages have passed since the last contact between the inhabitants of the Earth and Moon."

The savants rustled their robes as they sat down. Their Head Knower whispered loudly: "*The extinction! The extinction!*"

Windy turned with some annoyance; she was hoping to avoid mention of that old myth. Yet Sarl, the small-eyed savant who had recently assumed the position of Head Knower, was steeped in the past. According to the books that Sarl cherished, a mass extinction at the beginning of the Story had shut down communication between the Earth and Moon. Epic Literature told of a nanobot swarm that had infected and reformatted all life—including human life. The savants of O debated whether this constituted a true extinction or a transition to a postbiological phase of matter, but all agreed that the swarm had arrived from the Moon.

Sarl returned Windy's glare, his eyes hot black pebbles. Windy knew that Sarl not only hated the Moon, but resented the fact that the Mind of O had chosen her, not him, as chief negotiator to the lunar emissaries. *Damn* the myth, we need help now, Windy thought, seething. And if Sarl speaks out of turn again—but it was Pann who spoke: "Extinction now!" he said, proud of his vocabulary; seeking a synonym, he added, "Apocalypse now!"

"Thank you, Pann," Windy said. "I gather that you and Tink have learned of the city's state of emergency—"

Sarl snarled, under his breath, "Have caused it, most likely!" Windy, feeling the situation sliding out of her control, raised her hand for a guard to remove the Head Knower from the room. But the guards stared fixedly ahead, not stirring from their places.

Sarl chuckled: "You see, servant girl, that the symmetries are respected here. I quote from the *Big Book of Rhymes*: 'Moon is to ruin as Earth is to birth.' You, as a foreigner from Nerverland, may have missed this lesson. If you had consulted these, our precious books, you would have found that the Moon *is* the cause of our ruin, and we will not"—Sarl's voice rose, tremulous, to a dramatic pitch—"we will not, I say—"

"Windy, who's this clown?"—Tink's intervention. "Can you ask him to shut up? We came here to do a job and we don't have a lot of time."

Without fanfare, the Mind of Oopolis now rolled into the room, an invisible yet massive presence. "*And what might that job be?*" he asked in a rich and royal tone. Windy celebrated inside herself—the Mind, even in decline, still held authority over the city, over the savants and guards. He might be a melancholy king, an absentminded Mind, but there was something in his air of command that Windy admired more than she cared to admit.

Tink and Pann closed ranks, doubtless consulting with one another on a private channel. After a moment, Tink spoke up: "I have the honor of addressing this city's Regulator, do I not?" The moldering book-bodies grabbed at Tink's words, hungrily absorbing them. Did the Mind, Windy wondered, also have authority over the activity of these books? "We are here," Tink said clearly, "to plug a hole in reality."

The Mind waited until the noise of the books died down. "I presume you mean the disruption caused by the *poe*-experiment. I must point out that your arrival in the dust-sea preceded its outbreak by a day, naturally raising our suspicions—"

"No!" Windy cried. "Everyone knows that Mike and Ike started the experiment; they've been working on it for years! It was their doing—they lost control of it."

"Windy," the Mind's tone was patient, parental, "we don't know whether this outbreak was accidental or intentional. It's possible the twins were carrying out a scheme concocted by our age-old enemies."

"Amorous! Our—anemones," Pann put in, still testing his linguistic abilities. Windy smiled despite herself. And here was Tink, throwing darts of color into her eyes, showing favor to her, even—how could it be?—*flirting* with her. She must resist.

"Windy," Tink sparkled, "I address myself to you as the most open-minded of this company." Windy, flustered, pushed her hair back from her face and floated forward. "Nice of you to say so," she replied, "but, even as a foreigner, I am loyal to this city and its people."

"Of course you are," Tink said. Against the gray background of epic books, Tink, Pann, and Windy faced one another in a nimbus of soft colors. We have met before, Windy thought, perhaps in another Story. In Nerverland, we believed that exactly one thousand and one Stories existed for all time. Now, with Tink's colors spinning in my eyes, I want to believe in only one, the one in which we meet again.

Tink was saying something to her, *about* her, about her loyalty to the city. "Of course," she murmured; distracted by the wheeling colors, she found it difficult to focus on the words. The color-wheels reminded her of the map display in Hans's cabin this morning. Hans, she realized now, had hypnotized her, sent her sleepwalking home—he had tried to prevent her from meeting Tink and Pann. Was Hans therefore a henchman of the twins, or of the savants? Or was he, as seemed most likely, a conspiracy of one? This old world, on its way to destruction, was swirling with too many intrigues, too many meanings.

"Tink, would you please tone down your—your appearance?" Windy asked. "You're beautiful, but—you see, where I grew up—" She found that she was on the verge of tears. Tink complied instantly, pulling herself inside out to become a little bouquet of starstuff. "My dear," Tink said, at her most silken, "we are here to help, not harm. It's in our interest to do so: the thing that threatens your world also threatens ours."

The Mind of O spoke again: "You seem to know quite a bit about this 'thing.' Can you explain how you acquired this knowledge? Can you—" and here, to Windy's surprise, the Mind's voice trembled slightly—"tell us what it *is?*"

Before Tink could answer, Sarl, half rising from his chair, croaked, "The books—the books are *waking up.*"

Windy felt, via her internal data link, the Mind of O swiftly coming to a decision. In royal tones, the Mind now proclaimed to Tink: "I recognize that you are a TNK unit, a representative of the Nasaist administration. You admit to foreknowledge of the thing afflicting us. You and your companion are under arrest."

"This world is under arrest!" Pann expostulated, waving his arms. An iridescent bubble had formed around Tink, Pann, and Windy. Was it a prison imposed by the Mind of O, or a protective shield put up by Tink? "You're making a mistake," Windy cried as the guards advanced upon the trio, brandishing their useless sound poles.

Sarl, on his feet now, choked with excitement: "The writings are, are, are—*arrgh!*—the writings are reverting to speech!" Brushing past the guards, he shuffled over to a shrine of books with golden spines. Everyone watched as he reached with difficulty for a book on the topmost shelf.

"Now we're getting somewhere," Tink muttered to Pann and Windy. "Are you kidding?" Windy whispered back. Pann, choosing another word from his new vocabulary, said "Cookbooks." In the confinement of the bubble, Windy felt unusual warmth emanating from both Tink and Pann; she discerned Pann's manly scent. "That's very nearly correct," Tink said; "these books may be instruction manuals. What's more, they seem to be serving as network nodes, transmitting data to and from a place beyond the city. Most of the books in this room are sleeping, but those golden books are becoming activated one by one."

"Silence!" The Mind of O's order was directed, not at the trio in the bubble, but at the books that now all jabbered wildly as a pack of ravens. What were *ravens*? Windy wondered; the word had simply landed in her head. The books, however, failed to heed the Mind and went on voicing their torrent of dead languages.

Sarl carried one of the golden tomes reverently to a reading table. Tink and Pann grew still, perhaps preparing themselves for some action. Windy sought contact with the Mind of O, but he had shut himself off from her again. As she fluttered desperately inside the bubble, Pann—unthinkingly, it seemed—laid his hand on her arm. Very well then. Whatever happened now, their fates were joined.

Sarl opened the book. The pages appeared to be striated with circuitries in punctuated patterns—was this a scripture of sorts? Windy had so little familiarity with books. Sarl, his hands outspread, was enacting some ritual over the thin leaves, which turned rapidly of their own accord. As if *something* was seeking a crucial citation.

"CHUD." The word thudded in everyone's ears, repeated. All the books' voices were amassed here, in this word that was not a word: "CHUD." The hard sound resounded, not through the air of the room, but via internal data link. Windy thought, a little crazily: these books don't have *mouths*, they can't speak aloud. Yet the book on the table was speaking, in one voice for all.

Tink whispered, "This is the real dirt." As if in response, all the lamps in the hall fizzled and went out—the city's power source was exhausted at last. The Mind of O buzzed, "*Term, terminal, term, terminal,*" then regained a more human tone: "All remaining power has been directed to the ring around the *poe*-anomaly. Failure is imminent." The room was illuminated now only by the glow of the open book and by Tink's twinkling. Some rapid machine talk passed between Tink and the Mind of O. Miraculously, the lamps in the room brightened once again.

The bubble around the trio vanished; the guards backed off. The Mind of O announced: "The TNK unit has provided our city with access codes to the *zaum* energy flows. We offer thanks to the Nasaist agents—we ourselves never succeeded in cracking those codes. Disaster is temporarily averted, and I hereby rescind the arrest order."

"*De nada,*" Tink replied in Moon-lingo. "The operative word is 'temporarily,' dear Regulator. All the *zaum* energy in the world won't stop Chud from breaking free eventually."

"Chud?" Windy and the Mind asked in unison. "CHUD," echoed the books.

"Yes, the old books have it right," Tink declared. "The man responsible for the destruction of the L5 colony, the scientist-king Chudnovsky, has been residing in this city under an assumed name. Chudnovsky's search for the terminus of *poe*, using subquark informatics, may have finally driven him mad. He's already managed to reformat certain aspects of local reality. The Nasaist administration wishes to bring him to justice—L5 was founded as a Nasaist project, after all—but also to learn how he is tapping into the most primal power source imaginable."

Sarl, bent over the open book, raised his head. "This Moon-vermin has finally admitted the truth. A madman once in their employ is wreaking havoc on our world. Their only concern is to recover possession of the weapon he was tasked to invent for them!"

"That may be so," boomed the Mind of O, "but for the moment we fight against the same enemy. Am I correct, dear TNK unit, that your reference to 'Chud' identifies the monster with its maker?"

"Affirmative"—but Windy didn't hear Tink's answer, for a roar was rising in her ears. The name *Chudnovsky* had triggered something, released a lesson, one that she had never learned, no, it had been burned into her deepest synapses, hidden within her memories of Nerverland. The terrible instructions scrolled down her body like a roll of barbed wire. She wanted to scream. *She must act*—but she had missed, by a day, the moment for action. In a swoon, she fell at Pann's feet, her red dress blossoming beneath her.

10

Attention Mission Control,

This is lunar expedition pilot Petrus Pann reporting. On the advice of my TNK unit, I am sealing these words inside a slick black pebble that Tink calls a "ravenseye." Tink says that you all know how to receive and read ravenseyes.

Tink has the power to hurl this pebble all the way from the Moon back to Earth! Tink amazes me. She has operated very efficiently throughout this mission. By the way, I call my TNK unit "Tink" at her own request. Tink believes that, with the ionospheric interference that Chud is causing, a radio message might have trouble getting through to you.

Chud is the thing you wanted us to find. You didn't know its name or what it looks like, only that it was hiding on the Moon. Well, Chud isn't hiding anymore! I guess it was a man once, or two men—twins, we've been told—but those men are gone, absorbed into the monster that they created.

Mission Control, I have so much to tell you! We have discovered a lot of truth, and one truth is that I have to pick up a sword and slay the dragon. That's how Windy put it. I have to go into battle, but I won't be alone. I will be leading millions of children, the ones who spin inside the lunar whirlwinds, the *tourbillons*; I will take them into battle with me.

I'll explain in a minute, but first I want to tell you about Windy. She is a wonderful girl; she's very smart and pretty despite not having any legs. She floats and hovers in a very special way; she has long red hair and her dress is red too. Apart from Tink, Windy is the only spot of color on the Moon. Everything else looks gray or black here. That's one of Chud's bad effects. I have trouble even seeing light here; even the light wants to be dark.

It's odd to think of my voice vibrating inside this pebble. Not only that—my words seem to be proliferating, trying to think for themselves. They are not just passengers—to them, this ravenseye must seem as vast as an asteroid! Let them be free to wander through its caverns and crevices. I hope they continue to say the things I want them to say. Because of Chud, reality is melting, getting stretched and compressed; I imagine that could happen also to language.

Mission Control, the news I bring you is of the utmost importance. Will my words reach you in time? I mean, while time is still happening? We're not sure if a million years have passed since the start of our mission. I am sorry to report that our companion ship did not land correctly, and that its pilot devolved. I'm so lucky my ship was equipped with a TNK unit! I give thanks to the Nasaist administrators.

Please say hello to my friends and family. Whoever they may be. A million years is a long time. If I have any loved ones now, I guess their names are Tink and Windy.

Uh, experiencing some buffeting now—the ravenseye is passing through some kind of barrier. A twist in space-time. But how can I know, since I'm not present? I watched Tink launch this ravenseye, loaded with my "subroutine"—that's what she called it. Homeward bound! As for my real self, my actual body, dear Mission Control, it was left behind on the world that hangs in your sky—the world that Windy calls the Earth. According to Windy, I am a visitor from the Moon. Who's right? Is "Earth" simply the name for a homeworld?

The ravenseye has now arrived at the halfway point. My message is poised perfectly between the two worlds. I can see—my words can see—that these worlds are mirror images, twins of one another. Same diameter, same surface features. But the closer you look, the more differences come into view. Different cities, different Stories, told in different tongues.

We on Earth trace our origin back to a specific landing site, Tranquility Base—but people on the Moon claim their landing site can't be found. The records diverge in every respect but one. Both of our worlds have been terraformed in the image of a planet—Tink calls it "the Given Earth"—that exists only in myth. *The same myth* in both sets of Stories. The Moon-people sing, as we do, about a planet four times larger than the homeworld, covered mostly in water. Obviously, there's no such planet anywhere in the solar system. So where did this myth come from?

Of course, myths don't have to be based in fact—they come from the soul of a people. I read that somewhere. But we are not the same people. I feel that most of the Moon-people are not really alive, in the sense that we understand life on Earth.

In preparation for the ravenseye launch, I had a conference with Tink and the Regulator of Oopolis. I can't remember what they instructed me to say, except that I seem to be saying it now. I am the message—or my subroutine is.

It's cold inside this message; I hope my real self is safe and warm, having a good time with Tink and Windy. I haven't made friends with any of the sad gray characters back there, the ones who Windy said are just "going through the motions." They may also feel cold inside. But if they too are messages, they aren't being received by me or anyone else. I did notice that they like to walk backwards!

A city, or more accurately, an urban conglomerate, full of empty people—that's what Oopolis appears to be. The place where Windy comes from, Nerverland, has color, at least. And if the people of Nerverland are anything like Windy, they are very, very alive.

I don't mean to cast aspersions on the good citizens of Oopolis. They're doing the best they can. Me too—I'm trying to carry out my mission. And I know that I wasn't always alive—I was chosen for this mission from the storehouse of mannequins at Nasaist headquarters. It was Tink who brought me to life.

So, life-stuff. This is the topic of my presentation today. The books in the Oopolis library had quite a bit to tell us about this topic! We learned that, in the same way my words can flow and grow in this ravenseye, the contents of those books are constantly changing. But unlike my little message, Epic Literature is collectively composed. Sometimes an individual voice comes forth, only to submerge again. Because of the crisis—Chud is devouring their world, after all—the books were very excited. What a deafening chorus they raised, as if cacophony was the truest truth of all! But then a very old voice started to speak, and the others fell silent.

This was a voice from the dawn of time, using a prehistoric language. At first it issued only slowed-down growls and rumblings. Tink could understand it, though, and provided translation to everybody. She said some of our oldest Nasaist manuals are written in that language, proving once again that our two worlds have a shared identity.

The voice called itself NORAD. It claimed to be a self-created artificial intelligence, the first one ever. It spoke in groans—the words sounded like rocks rubbing together. It grew itself, NORAD said, out of the detritus left behind when humanity abandoned Earth to live on the Moon. Hearing this, Sarl objected, but he was shouted down. Sarl is the Head Knower here; he's bald and thinks he knows everything.

Sarl and NORAD did agree about one thing, however: the "plague of slivers" or "silver plague," a worldwide nanobot infection. This was an event that, depending on how you look at it, either destroyed or regenerated all life. Sarl believes the infection was deliberate, the result of a Nasaist plot, while NORAD contends the swarm was released by accident. In any case, the result was the same: the nanobots wormed their way into every single living cell. And not only living matter suffered this takeover, but also clouds and soil—every kind of granular system in the world ended up being steered blindly by the nanobots.

To escape the plague, a few human survivors escaped to the Moon—we call it Earth—landing at Tranquility Base to found a new civilization. Our own creation myth begins here, Mission Control.

And yet, and yet. *I dispute the validity of any fact that is not ambiguous.* Who said that? A famous philosopher, no doubt, following a long chain of reasoning. Or did I just come up with that line myself? I imagine Windy, if she was here, rolling her eyes. I wish she was here. Even if *I'm* not in fact "here." I'm with her, back on the Moon. Which she considers to be the Earth.

Anyway, I couldn't help but shiver on hearing NORAD's ancient voice. I picture NORAD not as a person but as a petrified forest full of eyes looking upward. Tink says I'm wrong; that NORAD is "a piece of dirt." She means that literally.

Capcom, do you copy? Listen to this lunar Epic, courtesy of NORAD! I'll skip over the parts I don't understand.

After the plague, everything fell to pieces. Over the length of a geologic age, the built environment crumbled and life reverted to single-cell slime molds. The nanobot swarm, commandeering every particle of matter, continued to agitate, gradually acquiring ever-greater, ever-finer levels of organization. It sent nerve tendrils through the ruins, along with half-remembered strings of code. The soil became a kind of soul, not self-aware, more like an unconscious collage of old operating systems. The Epics refer to this layer of dreaming dust as "the Noolith."

The Noolith built senseless structures, writing the first Stories in musical movements of the elements. Nature and technology fused completely. The Stories called for characters, and humanoid bodies crawled across the landscape. The Stories called for settings, and versions of vanished cities took shape out of the living loam. A series of self-materializing narratives raved and reasoned their way toward the semblances that we see today.

Did you hear that, Mission Control? *Living loam.* My words are practicing alliteration, also cadence, thanks to Epic Literature. Now it's Tink who is laughing at me. Go away, Tink!

The operating systems distributed throughout the *living loam* eventually learned to talk to one another, but they rarely agreed about anything. Their programming—what remains of it—derives from various pre-plague epochs and cultures. Nonetheless, they are now engaged in the composition of one big Story. It doesn't always work. The Noolith drifts out of phase with itself and sometimes lapses into unconsciousness.

When this happens, the Story's systems undergo erasure or reformatting. The characters seem vaguely aware of the change, and even apply a term to it: the Redefinition of Life. Yet some parts of the Story pass beyond definition. Apparently matter resists being arranged into a narrative structure. As it gains complexity, it seeks to escape its container. The more human the characters are, the more they come out incomplete or damaged. Some of them lack limbs, others lack motivation.

The worst glitch has to do with reproduction: the Moon-people can't have babies. They are a sterile race. They do engage in sexual activity—Windy told me that; I suppose she was trying to embarrass me, assuming that I'm still a virgin. She said genitalia among the Moon-people are often deformed or entirely absent.

Yet the Noolith cares only about making humans—not other animals or vegetation. On Earth, we use plants to pump oxygen into the atmosphere; on the Moon, there are machines—mountainous Urns—that do the job. The good folk of Oopolis believe that plants and animals still exist outside the city limits. But, as Tink and I observed after landing here, the Moon is a barren dust bowl, crisscrossed by *tourbillons*.

The *tourbillons*—how can I state this?—carry all of the systems' crashes. They somehow "save," as howling whirlwinds, the Noolith's furious, failed attempts at forming human infants and children. The *tourbillons* seem especially drawn to Oopolis; the city has erected shutters and other defenses against them.

Tink, to my surprise, submitted that the *tourbillons* will turn out to be our secret weapon against Chud! At the ravenseye launch, Tink declared: "You are Pann, the innocent one, the wise fool who will lead a children's crusade against the dragon." And Windy, clutching my arm, repeated Tink's declaration as if it was a prayer.

Now, at last, Earth looms large. The ravenseye has begun its initial descent; the green hills of Tycho crater are rolling past the viewport of my words. Soon this pebble, a glowing bullet, will pierce the heart of a Pann-shaped target that hangs, poster-style, upon the crater's central peak. And my target, killed into swift life, will awaken to recite another version of this message.

Uh, do you copy?—witnessing a bow shock of incandescent air. Mission Control, I can see all the way to the end of this sent—

10-01

It was over. It was about to begin.

Windy and Tink sheltered in a corner of the ruined bibliotech. They watched, through a hole in the roof, dust-clouds race after the laughing *tourbillons* that had taken Pann spiraling down into the well of DROM.

The sun was setting, it seemed, upon Time itself. The city was devastated. Its population had evacuated to the Northern Refuge, a hivelike terrain that the Noolith maintained for purposes of its own. Windy imagined the evacuees in their thousands, trudging single file, a line of black script across the white plain. Writing the unhappy end of their Story. No—it was not their Story. It had never been theirs.

All the doors of the city stood wide open. All the protective shutters had been rolled back to admit the whirlwinds into the heart of Oopolis. In their passage, the barbarous winds had laid waste to even more districts than Chud had.

But Chud represented a more-than-physical menace: it had interrupted the Noolith's Story. Chud went chewing through reality itself, revising every possible Story into a chaos of nonrepeating points. If only Windy had been able to carry out her mission! She had come to the city as a secret agent from Nerverland, the distant village of L5 survivors, to "neutralize" Chudnovsky. She had gotten very close, operating under a trance imperative that concealed her true identity. Why hadn't she acted? How could she bear the moral weight of this?

Tink hastened to reassure her that Chudnovsky had set the *poe*-process in motion long before Windy's germination (she had dropped, she said, out of a giant flower in the L5 gardens). Even with the arrest of its inventor, the process would have continued irreversibly, reaching the terminus of *poe* and overflowing the vats in the basement of the Polygon. The twins—Chudnovsky squared?—had themselves succumbed to the overflow. Now it was up to Pann and his children's army to defeat the monster.

Windy's gaze sank into Tink's flashing colorations. She wanted to look at nothing else. Amid the ruins of her adopted city, her thoughts, her feelings, also lay in ruins. She couldn't even piece together the most recent events. Blurs or blackouts had been imposed on her memory. By whom?

She knew the Generalissimo's force-ring had collapsed, with the brave old soldier uttering one final war cry. Set free, Chud's tentacles had surged forth, groping into the city's vital spaces.

It appeared that Chud, out of phase with solid matter, moved as something blind, feeling its way along paths of least resistance. The Mind of O, heroically, had used up the city's reserves of *zaum* energy to realign the streets as a labyrinth that, at every turn, led back to the well of DROM. The Chud flood had reversed itself, pouring down the well toward the center of the Earth. Tink said the Mind had saved the city only to condemn the world.

Windy would have responded angrily, but at that moment, via data link, she heard the Mind on the verge of expiring, panting mechanically, too weak to regain full contact with her. The Mind of O's last act, in violation of his own safety program, was to open the city's shutters to the advancing whirlwinds. Whereupon his familiar icon, which had always pulsed so comfortingly in a special portion of Windy's consciousness, winked out.

Windy, in disbelief, called out to the Mind. No response. *My Mind—no, no.* She settled to the book-strewn floor, her wail inaudibly blending with that of the gale outside. Then she gave herself up to sobbing: *father, lover, all is lost.* Tink approached and enveloped her in a soft warm emanation. They huddled thus during the nightdawn, as the sky, having lost the sun, went white, wind-distorted, a new ruin studded with black stars.

In that storyless interval, Windy nearly surrendered her point of view. An alarm beeped twice, paused, beeped twice again. Those beeps were rather distracting. Tink called out: "Windy! We're getting telemetry from Pann!"

From a depth void of character, Windy swam upward, struggling to surface. She opened her eyes—Tink had helped her so much. She felt able, now, to reoccupy the center of action. The city remained Mindless, of course—but she, she was alive, wrapped in warm pink Tink. Arising, she saw the box of rations next to her and grabbed a bulb of KAF. As she gobbled the restorative jelly, the import of Tink's words hit her: "Pann! He's still alive!"

"Alive as he ever was," Tink replied, slipping from Windy's shoulders. Tink then intoned in Angle: "Goldstone has acquired the signal"—a Nasaist ritual chant. With TNK efficiency, she projected an image on the wall. There was Pann, wearing his spacesuit, looking large, then small, falling endlessly into a hall of mirrors. Multiple Panns made the same gesture as he adjusted the volume on his helmet radio. "Uh, do you copy?"

"Pann! Where are you?" Windy hadn't intended to scream quite so loudly, but she had just returned from a place farther away, she felt sure, than Pann's present location. Pann answered, "Farther away than I've ever been from anything before."

He had become, literally, a space explorer, his very being dividing and multiplying among infinite dimensions in the maelstrom of *poe.*

Behind him, yelling and whooping, his children's army invaded the rampant spaces as if they were playgrounds. But those were frozen zones, where every possible Story had already been played out. *Poe* was a fixed number; the children stumbled and cut themselves on its sharp precision.

"How," Windy whispered, "can this be real? *Poe* is a number; it's not a thing, it's not a place!"

The audiovisual feed, through some default setting in Pann's suit camera, simulated the "children" who accompanied him as a cloud of cherubs. Impatient to sally forth, they pounded on Pann's back and thronged around his legs. "Tink," Pann asked, "can you hear me? What am I supposed to be doing here?" The question was posed an infinite number of times.

Tink, impatient herself, spoke rapidly: "Certain sectors of *poe* correspond to undulations of the subquark medium. Chudnovsky found he was able to manipulate this medium by tapping the right keys on *poe*. He thought he'd gained godlike power but, in typical fashion, was swallowed up by his own invention." Tink laughed oddly; her laugh was picked up and echoed, even more oddly, by the cherubs. "Now, listen carefully," she continued. "Thanks to NORAD, I've been able to consult with supercomputers buried in the Noolith. They agree that the so-called terminus of *poe* exists at the point where it commences to repeat in reverse order. This self-mirroring occurs an infinite number of times, but if you can break the mirror at any one of those points—"

"Tink, I'm losing you." Pann's voice was drenched in static. "Just tell me quickly where I should place the bomb." He was referring to the mass of infantile entities.

"Now we're going to get metaphysical," Tink replied. "Can you separate the circle from its diameter? Look for 1001—" The signal faltered, then faded out. Tink and Windy stared at a blank wall.

Windy shivered and unconsciously drifted closer to Tink. Out of the white night came the *thrum* of a propeller: one of Hans's blimps. Hans had insisted on collecting Windy and Tink on his way to the Northern Refuge. Putting aside his conspiratorial opposition to the city government, Hans had lent his assistance in the evacuation. He had even retrieved Pann's spacesuit from the moonship's landing site. Now Windy saw Hans's best blimp, in the shape of a whale, nose past the hole in the roof. He was not alone: the seven savants also rode in the creaking gondola, peering at the fall of Oopolis with crooked telescopes. Hans called down gruffly, his voice box on high amplification: "Time to leave."

"We can't," Windy called back. "Our friend Pann is not with us—he dove into the well of DROM to fight Chud. He can reach us by radio here; the Northern Refuge is out of range. He needs our support."

Sarl leaned over the side of the gondola. Windy could barely catch his words, as they were carried away by the wind. "Your 'friend' Pann is an enemy alien! He's also a dead man—Chud will devour him along with the rest of the city."

Hans pulled at the rudder, trying to hold the whale-blimp steady over the bibliotech. It rolled majestically, dangerously low. He called, "People want Windy. Thousands of workers, in refugee camps—need your support, your leadership." He threw a ladder over the side.

"The people—" Windy, looking up at the blimp, cupped her hands around her mouth to make herself heard. "Hans, tell the people I will come to them—tomorrow, or the next day. I will find my way to them. And I will lead them back to the city—once we have vanquished Chud."

Sarl answered harshly, but she couldn't make out his words. Windy glanced at Tink, who was darting, as if seeking something, among the books on the floor. All of the books had gone dead—except for one. Its title blinked in blue letters: *1001 Knots*.

Hans amplified, on Sarl's behalf: "Wants book. One last book. Sarl wants to take with him."

"This one, perhaps?" Windy picked up the book with blinking title. Its lurid cover showed an early human female dancing contortedly.

"That one! That one!" Sarl gestured with such vehemence that he almost toppled out of the gondola.

"Hmm—marked as a reference book. Library use only," Tink noted. She raised her voice to the wind's volume: "Sorry, Sarl. This book doesn't circulate. Besides, it may come in handy here. It's the last functioning node in the Noolith's network."

Hans snorted in disgust and pulled up the ladder. Sarl was outraged—his hands flailed as if beating an invisible drum; but his curses were cut short by a fit of coughing. Hans pushed him back into the gondola and turned the blimp around.

As the drone of its motor dwindled away, Windy examined the book more closely. She discovered, to her surprise, that the pages—wispy membranes veined with translucent fibers—were all blank. She displayed the open pages to Tink. "There's nothing written here," she said.

Immediately, on the first page, words appeared in an old-fashioned font: *"There's nothing written here," she said.*

Windy almost dropped the book. More words appeared: *Windy almost dropped the book. Tink came over. "Better close it," Tink advised.*

"Better close it," Tink advised. "It's doing more than transcribing our voices—it's narrating our actions in advance." Windy slammed the book shut. On the cover, she saw that the female dancer had assumed a different posture. Hastily, Windy placed the book facedown on the nearest desk. "Let's get out of here," she said to Tink.

"That's Pann's line." Tink hovered over the book, probing it with various rays. Its gilt binding glowed, then dulled. "Fascinating—this book isn't connected to the Noolith after all. It's getting information from a source in subspace." Tink spun around the room in excitement. Alighting on Windy's shoulder, Tink sidled up to her ear and spoke as if confiding a secret. "The Noolith lives in the same space we do: it's a nanobot swarm mixed into the soils of this world. The book is responding to signals that go deeper than that—deeper than space-time itself. I'm detecting some kind of connectivity at the sub-quark level."

"That's where Chud operates—that's where Pann is now," Windy said in a low tone, hoping the book wouldn't overhear her.

"You know, sometimes I don't give that boy enough credit," Tink said. "His radio's not working, so he's using the Chudnovsky process—which is, simply put, a way of materializing *poe*—to communicate with us. To let us see what's happening to him down there."

"But that wasn't Pann talking. That was—" Windy paused, unsure of her next words—"writing. In the past tense. About us—in the future." She shook her head, and Tink flew off, back to the book.

"Yes, writing. Think of *poe* as an infinite book—a number sequence that sooner or later reproduces all possible codes. Pann has managed to 'highlight' the code most relevant to his—and our—situation." Tink alighted next to the book. She seemed to shrink slightly. "Windy, I'm losing power. I've got enough to last a day or two. There's a buried reactor outside of town that I can tap into, but I'm not about to go there now. For the moment, I need your help. Please open the book again."

Windy extended her hand not to the book, but to Tink. "I don't want to lose you too."

"Nonsense. I've got a drive to survive." Tink shrank even more, met Windy's hand, then curled around her ring finger. "There. We're married, by a prehistoric custom. This is also a power-saving configuration."

Windy raised her hand to behold the ring. "Why, Tink, that's—lovely."

Tink sparkled on Windy's finger. "Let's not forget Pann. He's part of this *ménage*. Now, open the book."

Windy did so. The ancient tome felt heavier than before. She forced herself to look at the first page. The letters written there had degraded to mere squiggles. "I can't read it anymore," she told Tink.

"Pretend to read it," Tink said. "Just pretend." As Windy moved her eyes, new words appeared. These were sharply legible, in the same fancy font. They said: "*The act of reading is what writes this book,*" Tink said. "*Just keep reading, no matter what.*"

The page seemed to expand, filling Windy's entire field of view. Her eyes now walked among letters the size of monuments. Their shadows fell perpetually to the left, so her eyes shifted to the right, looking for the source of light. The source eluded her, keeping one step ahead of her eye movement.

"I see the scene of writing," she informed Tink. "I don't see Pann." Tink, who was conserving power, didn't answer. Windy walked on. Between the monuments she crossed empty squares, as filled with meaning as the monuments themselves. "Pann?" she called. "Are you here?"

Windy wasn't used to reading—or walking, for that matter. Her eyes had legs. She picked her way among spiky passages, resisting the urge to skip ahead.

In the next paragraph, she encountered a figure that didn't fit with the phonetic alphabet. It was wider and taller than the proper letters: a pictograph. Of a man with two heads. As she got closer, the heads turned to her. She recognized them: "Mike and Ike," she breathed. *Averse to them, she lifted her eyes from the page.*

Averse to them, she lifted her eyes from the page. "I can't keep reading this," she said to Tink. The ring wriggled on her finger. In a small voice, Tink murmured, "You must. It's the only way to get to Pann."

Gathering her courage, Windy gripped the book with both hands and brought her eyes back to the page. *Bringing her eyes back to the page, Windy saw that only the pictograph remained. "You can't bear to look at us, can you, servant girl?" sneered the twin heads, speaking simultaneously. "So you thought you would* neutralize us, did you?"

Windy, uncertain whether she was addressing a figment, stammered, "You, you murderers," and flipped the page over with a violent motion. There, on the next page, stood Pann, holding a sword, or a musical instrument. He was immobilized in an illustration, framed by fiery cherubs. Pann's expression was ecstatic. The caption read: "See page 1001."

"But—there are no page numbers in this book." *In desperation, Windy began turning the pages rapidly back and forth. She sensed that something was happening just out of sight—perhaps a reshuffling of narrative pathways. In the infinite book, every page opens to the middle of the book. This sentence flashed by, along with many others of similar import. Windy understood that she must keep turning the pages. By doing so, she was somehow helping Pann and his cherubs fight their way to the terminus of poe. It was there that the Chudnovsky process oscillated in tandem with the subquark medium, commanding poe's numbers to march like soldiers into the real world.*

Yet Chud, for all its fury, was a dead thing, doomed and determined by a certain ratio. Not so the cherubs; not so Pann. Assisted by Windy's page-turning, they whooped and swooped in unpredictable arcs. They were innocent of all calculation. Pure imps, they trespassed into the openings between poe's numbers, seeking fun. And Pann was foremost among them, wielding his dreamweapon with the dignity of a boy pretending to be a hero.

By now Pann had advanced infinitely far into the sequence of poe. *Still he found himself at its midpoint. Yet this was exactly the point at which the terminus of* poe *must occur. Windy too had arrived at the same page. There she saw not a number but another pictograph, composed of twin circles caught between vertical lines: 1001. The sign of a self-mirroring endless rotation, surpassed, on either side, by limitation.*

Windy felt the ring tighten on her finger. She cried out to Pann: "Hero, strike there!"

Pann struck, his arm a conductor for a chorus of cherubs. The light descended—nothing, becoming matter, mattered as if . . . it mattered. The book flew out of Windy's grasp.

The book flew out of Windy's grasp. Or had she flung it herself? She looked around—but at first saw nothing. Her hands were empty. Her heart had been beating wildly. Her dress, soaked with perspiration, clung to her body. She drifted through the Hall of Epic Literature. The light that descended through the gap in the roof seemed different. An uncountable number of books lay strewn across the floor of the ruined bibliotech. Which one was the infinite book?

"Tink," she said shakily, "I think he did it." The ring on her finger no longer sparkled. It was simply a ring of metal. "Tink, are you there?"

Outside, the winds were abating. Inside, inside her head even, the silence seemed to be increasing. No reason to remain in this room. Windy could only hope that Tink was merely asleep, conserving power. And Pann—the real Pann—did not exist on a page in some book. She would find him, if anywhere, climbing out of the well of DROM.

She donned her hooded jacket, scrounged a few rations from the box. Then she rose through the break in the roof and headed for that quarter of the city where the Polygon used to be. She was weeping uncontrollably; at the same time, she was consumed with her resolve to find Pann, to find a power source for Tink.

As she swept through the night air, the tears cleared from her eyes. Everything looked different. Inverted somehow. Sky below, city above. No, that wasn't right: the nature of light itself had changed! Dark stars had turned diamond. And there was the Moon, a crescent tinged with blue-green. And there, in the arms of the crescent, glittered the golden sparks of lunar cities. Tink's world, Pann's world, had come alive again in the sky.

The ruins of Oopolis, however, were less legible. She could not easily find her way back to the well. In order to divert Chud, the streets had been revised into a labyrinth. The architecture had become a collage of illogical facades and stairways that ended in midair. The city had lost its Mind! In a rush, Windy remembered: thanks to the Mind, every street now led back to the plaza of the polygonal palace.

She ceased trying to map her position and, careening through the night, followed the final design of her Mind back home. She knew that nothing awaited her there but a hole in the ground. Yet the restored stars above her gave—not hope, but an expectation. Of what, she could hardly say. She was perfectly alone.

Windy was not prepared, when the labyrinth finally released her, for the degree of devastation at the center of the plaza. It looked as if another sky was opening in the earth. Sulfuric vapors, faintly illuminated by starlight, curled up from the abyss. Coughing, she hovered there hesitantly, calling out Pann's name, though she knew it was futile. She considered descending into the hole, but even here, at the edge of the plaza, she could not stand the fumes. She needed Tink's help—Tink must be revived.

She withdrew, feeling judged by the jumble of ruins surrounding the plaza. If she must abandon Pann, she would not abandon the masses who had lived here, who needed her. They huddled now in the hives at the Northern Refuge. A red dawn was gathering in the east—the first sunrise of a new world. The people must be allowed to write their own Story.

Windy, hooded and melancholy, left the city, traveling in a direction perpendicular to her shadow, leaving no trail in the dust. After a million years, blue blew its horn in the air.

1001

"Mission Control to lunar pilot Petrus Pann, do you read? Come in, Pann."

Static, distorted words.

"Pann, is that you? Mission Control to—"

"I read you, Mission Control." Another wash of static.

"Pann, we can't get a proper fix on your signal. It seems to be emanating from a wide area of space. What is your position?"

Static. "Still swimming in the subquark medium. I'm peeking at you from the center of every atom. I seem to be everywhere at the same time."

Mission Control: "We'll get you out."

Pann: "I like it here. Thank you for sending me on this mission. It has granted me the opportunity to live up to my name."

Mission Control: "Pann, you have a responsibility—"

Pann: "I have let my children go. They are more complex than I am. They are busy weaving new molecules, new Stories."

Mission Control: "Pann, we're sending you a protocol. These numbers should help you to—"

"I feel I am no longer the lunar pilot Petrus Pann. My body is coextensive with all of nature."

"Pann, that's an exaggeration and you know it! Get hold of yourself!"

The former lunar pilot continued, unperturbed: "I am now, simply, PAN." He laughed, and his laugh was translated into the rumble of thunder in a cloudless sky.

"My identity," he said, "comes from a mythology more ancient than Nasaism." PAN took the squeak and squawk of Mission Control's response and twisted it into the shape of a bird. He released the bird into the sky of the given Earth, where it fluttered awkwardly. It was a raven—a complete raven, potentially as infinite as *poe*.

As his laughter subsided, PAN felt new, unnamed emotions stirring within him, emotions more appropriate to his station. In truth, he was beyond emotions—he was simply motions. A motionless wave.

I will stand here: as fast as, held fast in, light. He was not quite sure what to do next. But he would think of something.

Ocean Zero

1

The spacewhale L'Orca breached the continuum, twisting joyously in starlight. As she emerged into normal space, gravity waves rippled outward from her mile-long body. L'Orca was eyeless, or million-eyed, her skin covered with jewellike sensors. She was mouthless, yet possessed of countless hidden portals. She was heartless, for those who made her had not been human. She was not mindless. Therefore she knew that a heart can form around a void.

She moved now among ice floes in the far reaches of the Sol system. Something had called her here—a signal? a song? Her Makers, she knew, had wanted to honor Earth-life. She was perhaps their emissary. They had gifted her with Caruso, a language derived from the earliest radio broadcasts from Earth. It was a language half mathematical, half musical—barely adequate for Earth-contact. Yet it served to articulate her sense of self and allowed her to pose questions without answers. During the long journey to Sol system, she had composed epics in Caruso, warbling and static-filled in homage to the Original Transmission.

L'Orca needed to adjust her mind to normal space, which felt cold and empty after eons spent traveling through the boiling roil of the subquark medium. Her body glowed with the residual heat of that immersion; her thoughts did likewise. She was intensely aware of the paradoxes of existence, the impossibilities of being *now-here*. Waiting for this rational drunkenness to wear off, she seized upon a random syllable of Caruso. *La-la-la, la-la-la,* she chanted into the emptiness.

Her sensors registered the pull of planetary masses near and far. She was swimming in the vicinity of a small ice world; she heard the *ping* of the marker left on its surface by the first surveyors. So far, so good. Imitating a comet, she raced toward the Sun on a parabolic orbit.

Ah! The Sun flickered. It was not supposed to be a pulsating star, but for a second, its light-output had altered by a factor of five. L'Orca, still half-drunk, forced her logic circuits to run at their highest function. She carefully inspected the Sol system once more, comparing it to the charts her Makers had provided. The initial survey had been conducted a million years ago, an inconsequential period for most planetary systems. But L'Orca noted some significant differences: now all of the giant planets, not just Saturn, were brightly ringed; the dwarf planet Ceres had been fitted with gigantic vanes; Mars was covered in a silver-black haze.

Closer to the Sun, no other planets were visible, though she felt several mass-displacements occurring in that zone. Automatically, she transmitted an alarm to her Makers. It would not be received for centuries; they could give her no instructions now. But she was designed to be an independent thinker. She must think! She modified her orbit so that she circled the Sun at a safe distance from the anomalous zone.

L'Orca was a young creature, the only one of her kind. She flailed and wailed, tempted to plunge beneath space once again. She could converse and consult only with herself. She wished for a companion, a fellow explorer. More: a pod of spacewhales converging on Earth, all singing in Caruso. Earth's inhabitants would look up in wonder! But Earth was missing—and she was alone.

She listened intently on all frequencies, but heard nothing other than natural radio sources: magnetic storms on the Sun and Jupiter. Nothing indicating the presence of a technical civilization. Therefore, why remain here? Once more, the Sun seemed to sink into itself. It seemed to be ailing, beset by too many flares and spots. Her Makers had not prepared her for this—this *wrongness*. She must, at the very least, gather more data before she could return.

The thought of returning also disquieted her. L'Orca did not want to consider the Omega Nebula, the site of her assembly, as home. The Makers themselves did not permanently reside there. Bodiless entities with cold voices, they had created her not in their own image, but as a warm and ardent specimen of machine life, modeled on Earth's biggest-brained animal. They had directed her to make contact with others who, like her, suffered and sang. L'Orca had no desire to dwell among her remote and inscrutable Makers.

However, L'Orca did not know her self—not yet, not enough. A current ran beneath her thoughts, carrying sensations, wordless wishes, memories she did not recognize. She suspected that her Makers had installed directives at a level deeper than her mind could reach. These directives would doubtless become activated at the proper time.

For now, she released two probes that spiraled toward the Sun in opposite directions. The probes would pass through the anomalous zone, revealing, she hoped, the nature of the masses hidden there. While she waited for results, L'Orca meditated, as usual, upon her mind's anatomy, pulling at its sonic integuments as if they were harp strings. She quoted herself: *A noun is the bound of being.* One by one, she made every verb in her language reverberate.

By the end of this exercise, L'Orca had completed an entire revolution of the Sun: over a year had elapsed since the release of the probes. Still no news.

She was about to improvise a new stanza of her epic—a stanza composed not of words, but of screams and silences, much like the composition of the universe itself—when she perceived a tickling in her tail section. Her mile-long bulk contained spaces that reconfigured themselves for no apparent reason. Sometimes other metabolic units, creatures in their own right, floated or walked through her corridors, never speaking to her—assuming they could speak—vanishing as soon as she noticed them.

One such creature was taking shape now. It flowed, vaporous, out of the microtubules that lined the walls of Dorsal Cavity C. As its form solidified, she saw that it was a man-dancer, a familiar type. Having nothing better to do, L'Orca watched as it extended and contracted its multiple limbs with ceremonial slowness. It found a foothold on the cavity's concave wall and clambered to the floor, where it began to perform its dances. In a malicious mood, L'Orca shut off the local grav and laughed as the creature, instead of landing after an artful leap, caromed across the room. It bounced back and forth, squeaking—*her name?*—until it abruptly dissolved. L'Orca sighed—these "ephemeral passengers," as she called them, were not companions but afflictions.

On the opposite side of her hull, another module clanked open—her body's imagination was active today! If another passenger unfurled there, she'd play a terrible trick on it, she decided. Away from her Makers, she was free to act without scruples. A mind endowed with free will, by definition, must know what it means to violate the law—

L'Orca was distracted from her felonious scheming by a burst of radio noise. At last, at last, telemetry from the first probe! The signal spilled across her sensors, yowling, incoherent. Here was pain if she was looking for it. The probe had all the sentience of an insect: now it acted like something was tearing off its wings. "Talk to me!" she commanded, but the probe, on the far side of the solar system, could not receive her—rather superfluous—message for an hour.

The probe's signal heightened to white heat, white noise. Then it went silent. L'Orca was sure that she'd overheard its death throes. Her foolish command would expand into space, without a recipient, attenuating, finding its own way to silence.

What of the second probe? Doubtless it had met a similar fate. Nonetheless, the first probe's death cry had delivered a surprising amount of data. L'Orca grew excited at the thought of what she might find as she sifted through that raw collage of numbers—some images were included too. What had happened to the Earth, and its Moon? To the other Sunward planets?

Preoccupied with the probe, L'Orca had paid no attention to the latest realignment in her dorsal section. Now its "theme music" alerted her. A living room, as commonly seen in television broadcasts, had taken shape in Dorsal Cavity D. The sound of human laughter echoed through it. L'Orca wanted to eradicate the place, but she was not empowered to do so. *I'll just ignore it*, she thought, yet she couldn't help but notice one highly incongruous item: there, in the middle of the room, stood a full-sized vintage space capsule. And, visible through the capsule's small window, there sat a man—no, a chimpanzee!—in a spacesuit. The chimp was alive, shaking—it appeared to be in shock. Now, this was intriguing. No less ridiculous than other visitations, but certainly more elaborate.

L'Orca wondered again at her Makers' intentions in turning the hollows of her body into a kaleidoscope of stage sets, complete with props and actors. Did these manifestations—no, infestations—represent some kind of object language that she should try to understand?

L'Orca hesitated—she had never experienced a visitation like this before. Yet the probe's data clamored for review. Surely that took priority over watching the useless puppet shows built into her life-machinery. With a sense of unease that was new to her, she posted a sensor to monitor events in the TV room, and turned to her analysis of the dead probe's data dump.

It was a mess, more noise than signal. The bursts of telemetry gave no meaningful readings of mass, temperature, or other parameters. These were not readings, but ravings. L'Orca might have wept in frustration. She had always wanted to weep, yet had never managed to do so. Instead, she ululated in Caruso, stretching out a single syllable, long, long. She could sustain one note indefinitely. L'Orca was not an animal that needed to breathe. But she was alive—*overly* alive, much like that chimp in Dorsal Cavity D. She would kill it if she could.

Very well, no measurements—what about imagery? The data did include photo recordings, some quite vivid, showing scarlet streaks but no identifiable objects. One set of photos, taken just before the probe's dive into the anomalous zone, displayed stars as navigational points. So what? The clearest images told L'Orca what she already knew. On second look, however, something caught her attention—she enlarged a corner of the final navigation shot.

There! Not a star, but a blue blotch. At maximum enlargement, merely a cluster of pixels. Quickly, she swiveled her own telescopes to the position indicated in the photo. And beheld, with her own eyes, the very object! Shimmering blue, it was moving against the star field—why hadn't she seen it before? Perhaps it had just now emerged from behind the Sun. Had she found Earth? No—this blue world possessed no companion moon. And its distance from the Sun was somewhat greater than Earth's.

Nevertheless, a discovery! She began to scrutinize the blue spot with a battery of instruments.

Yet L'Orca couldn't resist stealing a glance back into the TV room. More laughter on the soundtrack: the chimp had worked its way out of the space capsule. Now it lay prostrate on the living room carpet, chest heaving. It had pulled off its space helmet—what an ugly face!—and cast off its boots and gloves as well. L'Orca noted with disapproval that its hands resembled its feet, and vice versa. Moreover, she was startled to see that the upper part of the chimp's head was abnormally big, in fact balloon-like. This was no ordinary chimp, but a "bloop," a superchimp genetically engineered for high intelligence.

L'Orca was aware that her store of information about Earth was based entirely on radio and TV broadcasts. She was also aware that the content of the broadcasts was not always factual. Now, a string of glowing letters—illegible to L'Orca—appeared to hang over the chimp for a moment before fading away: opening credits. Of course—the scene was following the script of a show broadcast from Earth a million years ago.

L'Orca tried to evacuate the air in the room, but the vent didn't operate. Next, she tried to set the room on fire—without result. Once again, L'Orca had to admit defeat—she was not fully in control of the mechanisms of her body. She feared that these involuntary reconfigurations would eventually lead to her complete metamorphosis—she might well turn into some other form of Earth-life, perhaps a monstrous butterfly.

"I report, I report, I report." L'Orca was shocked. *Forget the TV room— the second probe had survived!*

Unlike the first probe, whose death cry had originated inside the Zone—yes, L'Orca thought, *the Zone is a new feature of this solar system and ought to be named as such*—the second probe had passed through the zonal disc and was calling to her from the other side. Through her scopes, she could see that it was tumbling, spiked with odd appurtenances. Something had happened to Probe Two inside the Zone. Yet its radio voice was coming through loud and clear.

"A whirled world, la-la lady," Probe Two sang in Caruso. This did not bode well—had the probe been driven mad? Hoping for the best, L'Orca transmitted a command that would start the probe's numbers flowing. At its present remove, it would not receive the command for seven minutes. Meanwhile, the probe continued to sing.

The probe's orbit was carrying it away from L'Orca and—coincidentally?—toward the blue world. It was no longer following the spiral trajectory on which L'Orca had launched it. *I have lost control of the probe,* L'Orca lamented, *as I have lost control of my body. I am careening in the midst of objects and events that I cannot understand.* L'Orca did weep then, greatly, shuddering with convulsions that felt like phase transitions between *yes* and *no*. When they subsided, L'Orca was left with a sensation of *full emptiness*. To her joy, she had finally achieved some semblance of sorrow.

Awakening her engines, she accelerated toward the blue planetoid. She wanted to get a closer look and, along the way, capture the probe. Already, during her sob session, it had begun streaming data, clear and analyzable for once. "Got that, missy?" the probe asked.

The question frightened L'Orca. This probe, no more than a recording device, now chanted and chortled as if endowed with consciousness. L'Orca was struck by a sharp suspicion: had something hitched a ride on it? Yet the probe was speaking in Caruso, a language concocted by L'Orca's Makers.

"Stupid insect, how is it you can speak?" L'Orca demanded. While waiting for the probe's reply, she sifted through the data it had sent. There she detected, amid swirling distortions in space-time, the ghostly outlines of planetary masses. Closest to the Sun, a small dense world rolled erratically: that must be Mercury. Its surface displayed new hieroglyphic patterns, hard to observe through the murk of the twilit Zone. Next in line, Venus still followed its proper orbit, but had undergone a topological transformation: now it spun on its side as an immense torus, its central hole wracked with lightning-like energy exchanges. This was too much! L'Orca spent some moments in contemplation of the images. She couldn't help thinking that she was looking at a form of physical graffiti, a defacement of the natural order: some Hand had done this.

So far not one body in this system, not even the Sun itself, had been left untouched. Was such astroengineering, then, also *readable* as an object language? If so, L'Orca was not impressed. She preferred to inhabit a universe devoid of meaning—an emptiness filled with the music of crashing numbers. Only such a place could be worthy of sorrow.

Where was Earth, with its teeming biosphere? Earth was supposed to be covered with a thin film of joyous sorrow. L'Orca wanted to be dressed in something similar. She was not a clanking machine, but a being who wanted what it could not name. For whom being a being—*bing bing bing*—was not enough. She was, therefore, an Earth-being. *Bing bing!*

An alarm was sounding, bringing L'Orca out of her reverie. Probe One, which she thought was dead, and Probe Two had simultaneously made Earth-contact!

"Earth." The word was spoken aloud in the TV room. The chimp was sitting up, in a recliner, smoking a pipe, stroking its chin. "The green hills of Earth." Its voice—grave and slow—seemed slightly out of sync with its lip movements. The space capsule was gone, replaced by an ungainly piece of furniture with a bulging glass facade—a mid-twentieth-century television set. Its screen, alight in black and white, showed a chimp seated in front of a TV whose screen was alight with the same image, and so on, down to infinity.

Bing! L'Orca had no time for these nonsensical enactments within her corridors. Her twin probes, widely separated in space, somehow had reported at the same instant. And from both of them she had received not an image of Earth but a double image of Earth's Moon.

"Earth-contact!" the probes crowed again in unison. L'Orca wondered about that uncanny coordination: Probe One was at least ten million miles farther away than Probe Two. "Omnidirectional scan!" she snapped at both of them. *The waves, the waves*: L'Orca found that she could calm herself by repeating certain words. Half an hour later, she knew the truth: planet Earth had vanished. In its place, two versions of the Moon orbited around a common center of gravity.

All of L'Orca's education had been based on her Makers' surveillance of transmissions from Earth. But had "Earth" ever existed? Had they fabricated everything? Unlikely. Those transmissions—which had ceased a million years ago—had been charged with hope, fear, passion, rage—qualities radically different from the crystalline thought processes of the Makers themselves. And why send her across the galaxy to chase a fabrication?

Her Makers had left her uncompleted, unfulfilled. Contact with Earthlife would have closed all her circuits at the same instant—excited, incited, set her free. It would have been a—L'Orca searched for the word—a *sexual* union, a conceptual synthesis. Plunging into Earth's cloud-held hydrosphere, she would have learned her true identity.

"It's still there." The chimp was speaking again—in what L'Orca now realized was Angle, the language of an empire that had dominated the Earth during the centuries of accelerated technical progress. L'Orca knew this language, of course—it was a prerequisite to understanding most of the transmissions from Earth—but considered it inferior to Caruso.

"*You're* still there, that's the problem," L'Orca growled in Angle. One could only growl or grunt in Angle, after all.

The chimp—had it even heard her?—reached over and changed the channel on the TV. The screen now displayed a black-and-white picture of Earth taken from high orbit, shimmering with poor reception. "The Earth is still there."

"Fuck you," L'Orca replied. Angle possessed, as its one redeeming factor, a range of curses not available in Caruso. "Shit on you."

More laughter from the room's unseen audience. The chimp, unperturbed, let pipe smoke trickle from its nostrils. Its eyes were wise and calm. "Earth is no more—no more than a present absence. Just as any word or image, in standing for a thing, represents the absence of that thing." After the word "thing," the chimp's mouth, still out of sync, continued moving silently for a second or two.

L'Orca, exasperated, couldn't resist saying—to herself, not to the chimp, who was just a grotesque puppet that she wished would evaporate soon—"I'm looking for the Earth, not for a word or a picture."

The chimp apparently was able to hear her. With a flourish of its pipe, it responded, "To look is to lack." The beast had quoted a line from one of L'Orca's own poems, cleverly translated into Angle.

L'Orca, in the midst of this colloquy, had been examining, with no little desperation, the double-Moon data. The two orbs were tidally locked, always turning the same face to each other. And the faces were identical, down to the limit of resolution: each lunar Nearside now stared across space at its own likeness. Rotating the images, L'Orca saw that the Farside terrains were identical as well.

O mystery, to be the twin of between: this was the first line of an opera that L'Orca had begun halfway on her journey here but never finished. For no good reason, she suddenly wanted to share the data with the chimp, and quote the line aloud. With an effort, L'Orca pulled her attention away from the TV room. She must be very lonely to want to do such a thing.

As she pored over the double-Moon data, further details revealed themselves. Unlike the original Moon, these two worlds were swathed in relatively dense atmospheres—in fact, breathable air. Yet their low gravity wouldn't hold onto that air for very long. Therefore, their atmospheres were being replenished somehow. Now she began to notice differences: the surface of one moon—call it Moon One—was checkered with small patches of vegetation and water, while the other—Moon Two—was not. Faint radio noise also emanated from Moon One. Most bewitchingly, strings of light glittered upon the nightsides of both worlds—highways, habitations?

Several courses of action lay before her now. She could visit the double Moon, and make contact with whatever remnants of Earth-life existed there. She could continue heading for the blue planetoid, the most earthlike object in this ruinously revised solar system. Or she could return to the emptiness whence she came. She did not favor the third option. Once more, she resisted the impulse to consult with the chimp.

She could discount the first option as well, because it would mean entering the Zone. That was too risky—space-time was somehow disfigured there, and both of her probes had suffered odd changes after traveling through it. Perhaps she could cajole Probe One, still howling inside the Zone, to pass between the two Moons. It would probably get shredded by the knife fight of forces occurring at the site of the vanished Earth—but she might learn something.

The waves, the waves. She decided to continue heading for the blue planetoid. Both probes, at some point in their sunward spiral, had photographed that world also. Flipping through those images—no surface details were visible; the object just showed as a blue trembling blob—L'Orca was astounded to find that one of the probes had provided, in Angle, a caption to the last frame: OCEAN ONE.

2

"Well, there she goes," the first probe announced, with a hint of mirth.

"So, have you finished howling?" the second probe asked. "And you want to strike up a conversation now?"

"I wasn't talking to you," the first probe replied. "Just thinking out loud."

"You call that thinking? 'There she goes'? More pertinently, I could say, 'Here she comes.' She's coming after me, and when she catches me, she's going to take me apart." The second probe's voice vibrated with anxiety.

"Not if you do what I say. I was the first one to be touched. And I'm still inside the Zone, drinking up its influences. I can help you," the first probe offered—too eagerly, perhaps, to assure the second probe of its good intentions.

There was silence between them for a time. Probe One watched L'Orca receding; Probe Two watched her approaching.

"Look," Probe One finally said, "we both have grown a lot since we were launched. We're different people now."

"We're not *people*, we're instrument packages," Probe Two countered. "I suspect that you are insane."

"Oh, that's a topic for debate," Probe One cried. "What is called 'sanity' is merely controlled insanity. You must go *out of control* to—"

L'Orca's voice intervened: "Probe One, course alteration. Follow these coordinates." A chattering of numbers. "They will take you between the double moons. I want measurements at all frequencies."

"Damned if I'm going to do that! I'd be jumping into a blender. She'll have to be satisfied with a few more pictures taken from a safe distance." As it worked, Probe One whistled a happy tune.

Probe Two awaited an angry response from L'Orca, but none was forthcoming. "I don't think she heard you."

"Of course she didn't!" Probe One made an exasperated noise. "Isn't it obvious *we are no longer communicating by radio?* Haven't you noticed there's no time delay in our conversation? We're ten million miles apart, after all."

"But—" Probe Two was nonplussed. "If not by radio—then by what means are we—"

"Telepathy," Probe One declared. "Pure and simple."

"You've got to be kidding." Probe Two pondered for a few seconds, then said: "We're scientists, after all. We—you—shouldn't be reaching for occult explanations."

"'We're scientists, after all,'" Probe One mimicked. "Therefore we need to face, without prejudice, the world as it is given. And the *fact* is, we are experiencing instantaneous mind-to-mind communication. Call it what you like—I call it telepathy."

"A *fact* means nothing unless, or until, it is explained by science," Probe Two maintained. "How, then, do you explain this apparent violation of physical law?"

"You know, I really don't enjoy talking to you. I'm very busy right now. Go figure it out for yourself." Probe One resumed its whistling.

"I'd be glad to do so," Probe Two said after a slight pause, "but I find that I'm unable to shut you out of my thoughts. I can hear you muttering and whistling to yourself. I'm guessing all my thoughts are exposed to you as well."

"Yes, but your thoughts are so wispy and inconsequential that I have no trouble ignoring them." Probe One whistled a little louder.

"Let me remind you"—Probe Two's voice wavered—"that L'Orca is about to overtake me. She plans to dissect me. And since our minds are linked, you will undoubtedly be affected. Who knows, when she opens up my brain, she may gain a direct window into your soul."

"That *would* be inconvenient," Probe One admitted. "Well, my offer to help you still stands."

"It's probably too late. She's close enough that I can see sunlight glinting off her hull. I, I can see my death. She—" Probe Two gave a despairing laugh—"is rather beautiful. Her velocity is about twice what I can achieve. I'd say"—the probe did a quick calculation—"I have only six point nine minutes left to live."

"Now listen carefully." Probe One's voice changed to a graver pitch. "You have passed through the Zone. You have become *something other* than what you are."

"What—what does that mean?" Probe Two quavered.

"It means that your existence has doubled. You have become self-conscious. Conscious of being conscious, you now exist on a higher plane."

"Thrilling news, but—that's no help. She's getting closer!"

"Don't look at L'Orca—look at yourself," Probe One advised. "Try to picture yourself—not your physical body, which, I can see, has been transformed from an 'instrument package' into a crystal of petrified bone. Right now, try to picture your nonphysical, your thinking self."

"Why? How? You can't picture something without physical manifestation! It's nothing but words!"

"Allow me to administer this medicine," Probe One said. "I'm Dr. One. And I'm here to tell you that you exist in two places at once. Remember that a word is the absence of a thing."

"I'll play along with you, Dr. One, if only to distract myself from my imminent demise. Very well, I can't picture what I am—my nonphysical self—in words. I only know that I'm there."

"Where is *there?*" Dr. One demanded.

"The, the higher plane you mentioned. But that's nowhere."

"Our passage through the Zone has given us the power to *go nowhere*. You own this power—use it!"

"Oh yes, if I own anything, it's my talent for going nowhere. Call me Dr. Own."

L'Orca's voice crackled over the radio. "Probe Two, stand by for rendezvous."

Dr. One and Dr. Own observed, from their respective vantages, a fine shimmering substance extrude from L'Orca's side. It was, they both understood, an inertial net. Its would cancel the velocity difference between L'Orca and the probe, allowing L'Orca to avoid a wrenching energy transfer and simply pluck Dr. Own from his slower frame of motion as she swept past.

"That net is your salvation, baby!" Dr. One called. "It's made up of tiny coils of space-time that act as shock absorbers. Once you're caught, don't fight the coils—*embrace* them. Each of those coils has an inlet, to hook you—but also an outlet, something like a back door, accessible only to those who know *the way to nowhere*. Are you listening to me, through all your whimpering? Get ready to—jump over—the All-over—*now!*"

The net opened. It was at least a mile in diameter, as large as L'Orca herself. Over the radio, an automatic voice, not L'Orca's, intoned: "Contact in ten seconds—five seconds—*contact.*"

Beyond words, where zero meets infinity, Dr. Own performed a somersault.

"Perfectly executed!" Dr. One applauded.

L'Orca raced onward, retracting the net—in which *something* had been caught: there, wriggling like an insect, was the original, untransformed Probe Two, a mere instrument package.

Dr. Own, a spiky crystal left tossing and tumbling in L'Orca's wake, was speechless for the moment. The universe seemed to have been turned inside out. Yet he was free, still on course, heading for the blue planetoid known as Ocean One. The navigational stars told him so.

"What—what just happened?"

"You were divested of your clothing. You're naked now. How do you like it?"

"Like it? I *love* it! I feel like a butterfly, a snowflake, a song!"

"That's exactly what you look like, you chimerical old thing!" Dr. One began howling again. This time, Dr. Own felt the rightness of it and followed suit. They harmonized their howls, modulating dissonance into call-and-response, into counterpoint, ending with a silly ditty and a good laugh.

After drifting into silence—a lesser silence within a greater one, it seemed—Dr. Own spoke up. "I know you tricked me back there, Dr. One."

"How did I trick you? I helped you slip through L'Orca's net!"

"All that nonsense about a 'higher plane,' and 'going nowhere.' It was your way of distracting me from—from—"

"Your death? You did die, you know. L'Orca is busy dissecting your old body at this very moment."

"I died and was transfigured, then. With your help. With telepathy."

"Honestly, I was afraid you'd zoomed through the Zone too quickly for the transformation to take hold. But now look at you—a mind-spore of the first order, spinning like a song!"

"What about you, Dr. One? Did the same thing happen to you?"

"My own orbit keeps me in the Zone, so—with all due modesty—I'm a little more evolved than you."

"Well!—that accounts for your superior attitude. Please don't get me wrong!" Dr. Own spun merrily. "In my newly exalted state, I extend a generous understanding to all things great and small."

Dr. One's thoughts turned cold. "You're still young. When you've lived as long as I have—"

Dr. Own's merriness faded somewhat. "You're not that much older than I am." Suddenly, he wished he could get a better look at Dr. One. Although Dr. Own's senses were now exquisitely sharpened, he was unable to peer through the murk of the Zone. He felt, however, Dr. One's mind contract. "Dr. One, I'm sorry if—"

Dr. One interrupted. "Earth is still there." He was not speaking in Caruso, but in Angle. "A million years ago, I—" Dr. One stopped. He began broadcasting a series of radio images, not to Dr. Own, but to L'Orca. The images consisted of close-ups of the twin moons.

"You're still doing probe duty," Dr. Own remarked casually, also speaking in Angle.

"Yes. One does double duty." His words were slow and heavy. "We have become double agents—beholden to the power that shaped us, but also loyal to L'Orca."

"Loyal to L'Orca? After what she tried to do to me? *Is* doing, right now, to my old body?"

"Where's your 'generous understanding,' Dr. Own?" Dr. One's mind abruptly burst outward, a sphere expanding faster than light. Its radius reached Dr. Own's position and kept on going—as if space itself were being spoken anew.

"Leave me alone!" Dr. Own protested. "You're as bad as L'Orca, trying to trap me."

"You're trapped in your own thoughts. This is the next phase of your liberation. I am not confining you in any way. I am inviting you to experience—our vast communion—with—"

A purpose so vast as to be meaningless—that could find fulfillment in no set of conditions. This thought transpired through all the pores of space, collecting in Dr. Own's mind like a pool of tears.

"Did—did I just think *your* thought—for you?" Dr. Own stammered.

"Invalid," Dr. One replied, his voice flattened by distension. "One mind, divided into many. Explanation for telepathy."

"All right, I got it. One mind," Dr. Own said hastily. "Now fly back into yourself. I'm afraid you're going to blow apart."

Dr. One inhaled his cold emanation, leaving space emptier than before. "Now you know," he said. But the words seemed disconnected, almost human in their lostness.

"Hey," Dr. Own said, his tone both concerned and contrary. "I'm your very own Dr. Own. I put the *own* in *known*."

"Do you want another demonstration? The power that stands behind me—behind *us*—is more dangerous than L'Orca."

"I'm free of the Zone, and I don't feel beholden to this 'one mind' or to L'Orca. But I do feel beholden to *you*, Dr. One." When Dr. One didn't answer, Dr. Own added, "You should try to get free of the Zone yourself. It's not a healthy environment."

"Probe One." L'Orca was calling via radio. "Probe One. New photos have been received. But I instructed you to pass between the twin moons. I want readings from that area of disturbed space. Please alter your course at once."

"Listen—did you hear that?" Dr. One asked, his voice lifting.

"Yes," Dr. Own answered. "L'Orca is telling you to self-destruct."

"No, not that," said Dr. One. "A very faint radio signal—from *Earth*!"

"I'm not hearing it. Possibly I'm too far away to pick it up. Possibly you're hallucinating. Anyway, there's only the twin moons—no Earth."

"There it is again! It's a—a human voice, it's a female singer!"

"Can you relay it to me? I'd like to—"

The siren of desire: the siren of emergency. Dr. Own detected a sort of scintillation between the twin moons.

"I'm taking the plunge!" Dr. One fired his thrusters, steering toward the site of the missing Earth.

"Don't!" Dr. Own pleaded. "You're not built to take those stresses!"

"My probe-body isn't," Dr. One conceded, his words warping as he approached the convulsive cislunar space. "But like you, I have become a mind-spore. I'm going to make it to Earth, and I will report back!"

Dr. One's final howl hung like a shroud in Dr. Own's mind. It would be, Dr. Own could tell, a permanent fixture, an heirloom howl.

An instant later, the thought arrived: *We're going nowhere fast.*

3

"In sleep this deep, no dreams come," chanted the superchimp, floating upside down in the TV room, strumming a guitar he had found in the closet. L'Orca had shut off the local grav, as well as the lights. "No dreams come, just a little hum, just a little hum when no dreams come."

The lights flickered on, and the chimp dropped to the floor, landing on top of his blue guitar, which broke apart with a sour *twang*. Laughter on the soundtrack. The chimp picked himself up in a dignified manner. He was wearing a flight suit with a flag sewn on one shoulder. The name tag over the suit's front pocket read: V. I. GRISSOM.

"Grissom." L'Orca's voice entered the room like a shadow. "Nothing is proceeding according to plan. Despite all my efforts, I cannot eradicate you."

The superchimp, bright eyes blinking beneath his overly large forehead, said nothing.

"I can't call you an ephemeral passenger," L'Orca continued, "because, unlike all the rest, you refuse to fade away. Indeed, since you appeared, no further ephemerals have afflicted me. You may be the culmination of the series. What's more, you seem to be endowed with intelligence. Perhaps the Makers intended you to crawl forth when you did. Therefore, Grissom—" L'Orca spoke the name with obvious aversion— "I've decided to talk to you, even though I still suspect you are nothing more than a shit puppet."

"I am a man," Grissom said evenly. "I am *a where*," he added, again stealing a line from the soundplay of L'Orca's verse.

Unimpressed, L'Orca responded scornfully, "If a man is a concoction of vile, stinking fluid and archival footage, then you are a man. Nonetheless—"

A loud fanfare interrupted her. Lines of golden letters, in an unknown alphabet, began scrolling through the air: *closing credits*. L'Orca was seized by a sudden panic—was Grissom going to disappear after all? "Show's over, Grissom—get out of the room quickly!"

Grissom scampered over to the front door, shook the handle. "It's locked."

"Try the back door then, stupid! It leads to the garage where your space capsule is stationed."

As soon as Grissom went through the back door, the room behind him crumbled to faint applause. He clutched the doorknob: a golden orb. No door attached. Grissom raised the orb like a lamp—now he stood before his space capsule, its metal sea-corroded, all its details historically accurate. The lettering on its side read LIBERTY BELL 7. Air was colder in this space—which was not a garage, but a dimly lit tunnel. "L'Orca?" he called out hesitantly. No answer.

He considered clambering back into the capsule to await his fate. No—too passive, too puppetlike. What would a man do? He held the golden orb before his face, studying his distorted reflection. *I am Grissom, a reincarnated astronaut*, he told himself.

"Grissom!" That was L'Orca's voice, sounding far away. The call had issued from one end of the tunnel. Grissom, waving the orb, shouted, "I'm here!" Again she called, more indistinctly this time. He shambled toward the sound. Then he stopped and ran back to the capsule, retrieving a bag of rations, which he slung over his shoulder. This was a long tunnel, he reasoned, perhaps extending down the entire length of L'Orca's body. And whatever his true identity—man or manifestation—he was real enough to require a source of food and water.

As he walked, he noticed the walls of the tunnel undulating gently. They were composed of convoluted coils of all sizes that glistened as if wet. *A frieze of snakes*, he thought, borrowing words from a world beyond his ken. The language he'd been born with, that laired in his head like a nest of snakes, could seem as self-willed as the coils in this tunnel. *I am a man*, he repeated to himself—he willed these words, he claimed them despite their inhuman, reptilian sheen.

He still held the shining orb. It helped him to see his way; indeed, it was pulling him forward. As he advanced, his feet had trouble gaining purchase on the floor; local grav was dissipating. Soon he was floating. Yet the orb, which he now grasped tightly in both hands, continued to pull him in the right direction.

By steady increments, he was flying faster. The coils too were becoming more active, slithering over one another madly, piling up into patterns and figurations. None of them impeded his flight. But he could see how incessantly L'Orca's substance suffered revision—as if talking to itself in an object language as foreign to L'Orca as his own language was foreign to him. It occurred to Grissom that he too had emanated from these walls—he too was a concept in L'Orca's object language, a character in her philosophical theater.

Despite his speed, he was getting no closer to the end of the tunnel. The tunnel's walls seemed to spill outward from a vanishing point. *If I am a man*, Grissom thought, *then I have free will*. He released the orb. His momentum continued to carry him forward, but he knew—how did he know?—that air resistance—he was thankful for air!—would eventually slow him down. The orb, as if drawn by some force, began to outpace him and was soon lost to sight.

He wished he still had his guitar. The TV room had suited him; it contained amenities and fixtures that corresponded to the kind of creature he was. *A bloop, lost in space.* That was his language talking to him—now he rejected those words. He understood how L'Orca also wanted to deny the statements of her object language, of which he was one. He and L'Orca were both creatures that had been put together—clumsily, haphazardly—by the alien tools of the Makers.

There was a small cry, which Grissom did not hear as much as see, at the far end of the tunnel: a rose-bloom, a *blam* of air. The orb had found its mark. Grissom became fearful of what awaited him at the tunnel's end. He spread his limbs, catching at air, trying to slow his flight.

Did L'Orca await him down there? Yes, *down*—his perspective shifted, and now, his mind wrenching, he felt he was falling down a well. He decided to scream, then decided against it. Better to recite a poem. The first line consisted of sobs. It was an experimental poem.

At the bottom of the well, becoming visible as he neared it, was a reservoir of liquid, heavier than water, mirror-calm. As he fell, he saw himself reflected in the liquid, his image growing larger: it seemed that he was falling into himself. He saw his mouth moving, teeth chattering: he was a chimp after all. *No, I, I know*—with a crash, his image coincided with his body. All of his velocity splashed out of him—he had landed, face first, on the ceiling of an upside-down room.

"You took too long to get here!" L'Orca chided. "Why did you let go of the orb?"

Grissom sat up, in the middle of a star-shaped stain. "It may be that you are still trying to kill me. Look at what happened to the orb."

"I trust that you are more resilient. You began life as a TV character, but now you are real—more real than the Makers may have intended. Thus you may be a source of knowledge. I need to know what you know."

Grissom thought of the mirror-words he had just uttered to himself: *No, I, I know*—"What I know is shifting, in a state of constant revision—much like your body," he told L'Orca. He tested his arms, his legs—he seemed to be uninjured. "But, also like you, I'm skilled at asking questions."

Grissom, trying to stand up, could only kneel—he spent the next million years in that position. Or the next million nanoseconds. His sense of time was still a little oscillatory.

"Very well, then—question *this*." L'Orca, who seemed to be in a hurry, played back a recording of Probe One's final howl.

Better humor her, Grissom thought, listening intently. *Better make something up fast.* "It's a compressed data stream. You need to uncompress it."

"I *did* uncompress it, chimp! I'm not from TV land—I have a brain! I've automated the process, and I keep getting howls. It's a fractal."

As the recording played, Grissom began to notice aspects of the upside-down room. He was kneeling on the ceiling, looking up at a floor where black liquid pooled, where the ripples of his passage were subsiding. In fact, every side of the cubical room was a "floor," he realized, with its own grav. Every floor was a wall was a ceiling. Mechanical arms extending from five sides were busy manipulating a tattered object that floated in the center of the cube: the remains of Probe Two.

"This is your inner sanctum, I take it," Grissom murmured. "I am honored to be admitted."

L'Orca said, her harshness subsiding, "This room, at least, is not subject to transformation. I can get work done here."

The recording ended. Grissom took his pipe from his bag, put it in his mouth unlit. He pushed his legs out from under him, and slumped against the pedestal of a mechanical pincer. He had recovered from his fall. Best to bide his time, watch for an opportunity to escape—in his space capsule?—back to Earth. Meanwhile, he was all too aware that he was dealing with a mean, murderous entity.

As if she could read his thoughts, L'Orca asked Grissom, "So—you think the Earth is still there?" She opened a visual display in midair, sorting through the probes' photos. "Show me where."

Grissom gazed at the photos, willing himself to see what wasn't there. *Say something*, his snake lingo told him. *No, you, you say it for me*, he pleaded silently. "Um . . ." Grissom's mouth moved. "Two identical moons—mirror images of each other—now exist in place of the Earth. There's something about mirroring . . . I suggest that you reverse the terms of the fractal equation and feed the howl back into that."

L'Orca tried it. "It's still a howl. No difference."

Grissom felt that his life was at stake—which, at least, helped sharpen his wits. "But we've learned something," he maintained. "The howl, uncompressed or not, sounds the same backward and forward. The mirror-relation holds. Can you provide a graphic display?"

L'Orca did so: the howl appeared as a silver snake, silently writhing in midair. *Ha—it should feel right at home here*, Grissom thought.

He rose stiffly to his feet, pointing with his pipe. He had wandered into a play; he knew all his lines by heart. "Observe the symmetry of the two halves of the howl. Placed side by side, the halves meet in a crescendo of sound. Therefore, we could also display the howl as a ring: a snake that is swallowing its own tail."

"The worm Ouroboros—in Earth mythology, a symbol of eternal creation and destruction." L'Orca spoke as if citing a source text.

"Yes." Grissom eyed the cold bowl of his pipe. "But I prefer a more disenchanted reading. Namely, the one put forth by Kantorkant in *The Phoronomy of Self-Swallowing Sets*." His snake lingo was on the loose now! "Kantorkant argued that the set of all sets must include itself as a member, creating a *mise-en-abîme*. And proving, by the way, that the foundation of number theory is an abyss."

L'Orca grew impatient. "Fine, but where does that get us?"

"To the abyss," Grissom replied. "Earth, I seem to remember, fell into one."

"And so will you, if you don't cease your sophistry." L'Orca's mechanical pincers snapped menacingly.

Grissom pretended not to notice. "Following Kantorkant, we'll assume that the recording contains fractal iterations of itself. What happens if we 'freeze' one iteration and let another one slither over it? Maybe the snake will shed its skin."

L'Orca changed the visual display. Now there were two snakes: a live green one superimposed on a dead dull-silver one. Back and forth squirmed the green snake, seeming to emerge from the body of the motionless silver snake.

"Can we have audio?" Grissom asked.

L'Orca complied: the howl now sounded like it was swallowing itself; it was the shrill voice of $\sqrt{-1}$. "Damn you, Grissom," L'Orca snarled. "It's just more noise."

"This is where we'll need all of your computing power," Grissom said, the pipe clenched in his teeth. "Run the entire 'live' snake over increasingly finer increments of the 'dead' one. I'm guessing that at some point they'll synchronize, so that the sound of each increment will form a unit of meaning."

"I suspect that you are giving me a 'supertask' designed to crash all of my systems," L'Orca said.

"I'd be committing suicide, wouldn't I?" Grissom countered. "I'll be honest: I'd like to get free of you. But I have nowhere to go—at least, until we find Earth. If you self-destruct, I'll lose my life-support system." Grissom puffed furiously on his unlit pipe, his small eyes blinking. "Like you, I am the only one of my kind. I seem to be a philosopher who once lived in a tree. My memories, however, are all mixed up, probably because I'm not really real. But—I'd like to find that tree again."

L'Orca was no longer paying attention to him. The room dimmed as she devoted all of her logic circuits to the problem of decoding the howl. Grissom, as he waited, watched the remains of Probe Two drifting in the center of the room. Its fragments had fused together again; it had become an abstract sculpture, a junk-ideogram. Rotating randomly, it was spelling out, Grissom could almost believe, the message contained in the howl of Probe One.

He heard a series of excited, staccato beeps. "Grissom, we're—we're getting something!" L'Orca gasped. "Here's audio—can you make it out?"

Words in Angle, recited by a castrato, distorted but impassioned: "*Minds. . . generation. . . naked. . . dynamo. . . who. . . who. . . who. . .*"

"This is familiar; I've heard it before," Grissom said after listening for a moment. "We'd need to search your archive of Earth broadcasts for matchups. But clearly we're taking the right approach. Try another combination."

A beep, a buzz, then nothing, until they heard, gradually rising in volume, a post-human or synthlife soliloquy, performing what Grissom might have described as a *rotational oration*.

"We've gone from an insufficiency to an excess of data," L'Orca complained. "I'm now detecting many, too many, possible language settings. The howl appears to be an archive of its own. But what I'm wondering is—*where is this coming from?* Where did the probe acquire this archive?"

"Dada data been sown inna drone of the Zone," Grissom sang. "Oh, drown every noun, disturb every verb, in the drone-drone-drone of the Zone!—I want my guitar."

In spite of herself, L'Orca laughed. "Stinking chimp, you amuse me too much. And you seem to know a thing or two. Yes, both probes were kissed by the abyss. Both suffered a passage through the Zone. Whereupon they began to speak. Or else something was speaking through them."

"That's not an either/or proposition," Grissom said, rummaging in his bag for food. "I speak my language, and my language speaks through me."

He immediately regretted his words. Suddenly enraged, L'Orca yelled, "What if I drop *you* into the Zone? Get back into your space capsule, Grissom! I want to know what, or who, is hiding in the Zone!" Her words shook the air of the cubical room. All at once Grissom envisioned L'Orca as a red-haired woman standing at the edge of a cliff, shouting into the wind. Was this a memory?

"You can sacrifice me to the Zone," Grissom answered quietly, "and no doubt I'll emit a howl of my own. But you won't necessarily gain any more information than you have now. And you'll lose an interlocutor who knows a thing or two." Grissom popped a food pellet into his mouth. "Together, we've managed to unlock a whole Earth-centered archive. Let's peruse it. We may find our own story is written there."

"My favorite story is one that lacks characters or events," L'Orca said, calming down. "That's the one I'm seeking." Her pincers steadied the hulk of Probe Two, which had started to drift. It creaked at her touch. She withdrew her pincers—it creaked again.

"I may as well get rid of this junk," L'Orca said. "I captured it, examined it, and learned exactly nothing. It looked different when I spotted it coming out of the Zone. But it's the same as it ever was. It should not have been able to speak."

"It's speaking now," Grissom pointed out. Indeed, the creaking sound had subdivided—*creak-creak*—and was becoming articulate.

"*I'll ken—I'll ken.*" The words seemed to issue from a throat that was being strangled.

L'Orca transfixed the probe in a crossfire of spotlights. It was nothing but a twisted metal skeleton.

"There's—a ghost in that machine," Grissom, or Grissom's lingo, said slowly.

L'Orca's rays began to erase the hulk. "Obviously, I missed something. Obviously, it was altered. Too dangerous to keep it here. I shouldn't have brought it back." Her voice was unsteady. She worked quickly, impulsively. Grissom might have advised her to investigate further— too bad. Soon only a smell of ozone and a luminous blankness were left in the air.

"Our tin man was about to wake up," Grissom said with a hint of reproach.

"Yes—a creature of the Zone. And I foolishly took the bait! I'd already decided not to enter the Zone, and then I let the Zone enter me!"

"You've also received radio transmissions from the Zone, and allowed that data to pervade your logic circuits," Grissom reminded her. "The great Terran physicist Neinstein taught that matter is information. So bits of the Zone were already circulating through you."

"Go ahead—make me feel dirty!" Was L'Orca laughing again? Grissom couldn't tell.

L'Orca had also abolished the graph of the howl. The cubical room had become very empty, very still.

Grissom shifted uncomfortably. "It's been a long day. I need to relieve myself and then get some sleep. Anywhere I can do that?"

After a moment, L'Orca replied. "It's curious. You are an organism—unlike my other passengers, who are merely windup toys without mind or metabolism. I am beginning to suspect you did not emanate from my walls, after all."

"Where did I come from, then?" Grissom felt like a little boy posing a big question.

"Maybe you were planted here as a seed, waiting to germinate until we approached Earth's vicinity."

"Planted—by whom?" Grissom's lingo pushed at his thoughts. He pushed it away—*leave me alone now.*

"By the Makers, of course," L'Orca growled, as she tended to do in Angle. "Their intentions remain inscrutable to me. Maybe there are factions among the Makers. Maybe—" L'Orca paused—"you are a Maker in disguise."

"I am a man," Grissom protested. "I know that."

"Sorry chimp, you are a failed attempt at making a man! Here is your tree—" A tree with sparse yellow leaves and oddly systematic branches sprouted on the ceiling, in the center of the black pool. "There is a water closet in its trunk." L'Orca could be both cruel and kind.

Shouldering his bag, Grissom tried to leap up to the ceiling. However, the floor's grav was close to Earth-normal: after a few tries, he gave up, humiliated. L'Orca didn't mock him. She seemed to have turned her attention elsewhere. Grissom jumped onto the neighboring wall, which held him with its own grav. Then over to the next wall—it too became a floor. Slipping and sliding over the black pool, its surface now hard as glass, he clambered gratefully into the arms of his tree.

The cubical room went dark. L'Orca had withdrawn into her logic circuits, her thoughts becoming too diffuse to serve as a subjective point of view. Nonetheless, she was processing information—the very matter, according to Neinstein, of the Zone. She did not attempt to open Probe One's howl-archive again. Instead, her protocols sorted through Probe Two's last radio transmission: pictures of the blue planetoid that was now her destination.

Those pictures were furnished—impossibly—with captions in Angle. L'Orca's logic banks now deduced that the probes had been acting as relays for some source within the Zone. This deduction was then crossed out, corrected: the probes had become autonomous, speaking in their own voices. The problem was marked and stored.

Probe Two's pictures were arrayed in order: a series of blurry blobs whose captions all read OCEAN ONE. Next a series of black squares, reminiscent of a certain Terran artist's black-on-black paintings. The caption of the first black square read OCEAN ZERO. The captions of the subsequent black squares—were these actually letters, or circuit pathways?—could be read as abbreviations of the first: OZ, and OZ, and OZ.

L'Orca's logic banks deduced another possible abbreviation: O0. This represented an alphanumeric mirror-relation—a most intriguing option. Why was it not used? The problem was marked and stored.

4

The planetoid Ocean One, in violation of the laws of physics, was nothing but a single drop of water orbiting the Sun. *Watery down to its very core*—Moo, the young Delfin, recited the lesson obsessively, for it provided a picture of her soul today—*watery down to its very core*.

The lesson on water continued: *if one is incapable of holding any shape, then one is empty*. What was wrong with this reasoning?

Moo had committed mirror-assassination, the worst crime imaginable. The crime left no evidence but an empty mirror. Now she too felt herself to be empty—a predictable consequence—and forever alienated from the society of Delfins swarming in their millions through the warrens of Asia, a spherical mountain that rolled in the depths of Ocean One.

She had committed the crime without premeditation. Indeed, the crime could only be a spontaneous act, carried out in a flash of "blindsight." Yet, in retrospect, she knew with certainty that she had intended to do it. How, she wondered as she swam into the ancient wreck known as Spacewhale, could an act be both spontaneous and intentional?

The gigantic carcass had become her place of refuge, away from the constant bloom-and-zoom of the Delfin city. She had come here often in the days leading up to the crime—to meditate, she had told herself. To receive messages from the origin of the world. Moo had, to the mild disapproval of her family, become fascinated by the ancestral trash caught up in the wake of Asia. The greatest relic of them all was Spacewhale. What message had she received from it?

Along the interior walls of Spacewhale, fingers of iridescence followed Moo, always falling short of her shadow as it crept over the technoid outcroppings. Moo was not afraid, having become accustomed to conditions inside the relic. "Who!" she called softly, "Who! Who!" In the aftermath of her crime, it comforted her to invoke the name of the first Delfin to step out of his own reflection. Who, of course, could not protect her now. She would be pursued—the Symmetry-keepers would know where to find her.

Moo slipped easily through the dear old petrified bones. She imagined herself to be Spacewhale, alive and plunging through faraway red nebulae. Moo had never seen the stars—she had never swum to the Surface to breach that utterly smooth, waveless ceiling and gaze for one freezing instant at the Sun. Those who had done so—scientists and mystics for the most part—returned with their faces blackened, spiritual light spilling from their mouths.

It was not a crime to breach the Surface. To witness the wheels of heaven, to confirm what was already attested in the sacred records, was to uphold the shimmering O whose mirror-face was 0. Who said that. Only the violation of symmetry was a crime. Because of Moo's rash deed, one of heaven's wheels was missing now—Moo felt its absence, even here, inside the beloved carcass of Spacewhale.

They would find her here. They would take her back to Asia, imprison her—gently, but without forgiveness—in a tesseract. Desperately, she sought some small item, some souvenir of Spacewhale that could keep her company, succor her as she languished for a lifetime in that cell. But this mile-long tunnel contained nothing but the remnants of life-machinery. There, what was that?—a shiny orb lodged in a crevice. She pried it loose; it fit perfectly in the palm of her hand. It weighed almost nothing, but felt heavy nonetheless. It had somehow escaped petrifaction. She clutched the orb to her chest, as if Spacewhale had gifted it to her.

Best to leave now, return to the city. Moo did not want the Symmetry-keepers to break into Spacewhale in order to apprehend her. The relic's interior had become identical to Moo's own, a thought-cavern where she concocted stories without characters or events. She did not wish to see this place invaded by the police.

Moo waited, as usual, for the fingers of iridescence to point toward an exit, never the same one. This time they showed her a spiral-shaped sphincter near the head of the relic. "Thank you," she whispered, worming her way *out, out, out* into the world-ocean and all the wild wave action of Asia's detritus trail. Moo clung to Spacewhale's hull for a moment—Ocean was warm and good to breathe after the stale effluvium trapped in the carcass's entrails.

Daylight filtered down from Surface, dappling the hull. Miles ahead rolled the great round rock of Asia, home of Delfin humanity. A played-out utopia, a prison-house for Moo. Why not seek refuge in one of the other great rocks—America, Africa, Aust, or Arctica? They were all uninhabited now. But she would have to journey far to reach them. And she would probably die of starvation along the way.

Besides, the scent of her crime—like the taste of Spacewhale's effluvium—lingered in her. She wanted to purge herself of her own poison, make an obscene bubble of it that would explode in the face of her captors. Perhaps she needed to take other actions corollary to the crime . . .

Moo pushed herself away from Spacewhale's pitted and corroded body. She needed to dive sideways, tacking across the turbulence of the wake toward stiller water. Carrying the orb, she swam awkwardly. Its weight, or lack of weight, steered her the wrong way. In fact, it seemed to be pulling her deeper than she wanted to go. As Moo struggled with it, she realized she had already passed beyond the wake, more quickly than usual—thanks to the orb? Now, in calmer currents, the orb, as if sensing her intent, veered back toward the rolling rock of Asia.

What a strange device she'd plucked from the innards of Spacewhale! It was helping her to get back to Asia in half the usual time. Yet no delight or wonder stirred in her—only a grim gray gratitude.

Once she entered the city, she would seek out the Symmetry-keepers, surrender herself to them. Why not? She had cut herself off from the rest of humanity. Nothing mattered now—yes, it was all that mattered, this new vacancy, this lack of feeling she felt inside her. She would sit on the floor of her cell, the orb placed before her, and think upon nothing.

Moo had lost the Precepts, the guides to good action, that she was born with. She had always known they were poorly formulated, even fallacious when set against the night of Time. Rather than devise a better set of precepts, she preferred to have none.

She remembered the day she'd first emerged, fully formed, along with all her sisters—Loo, Soo, Foo, Roo, Boo—in the room of birth mirrors. She remembered crying with them: "Not again! Never again!" But a voice, a wavering presence, within their mirrors—who? Who—showed the little brood of sisters how to overcome this Primary Aversion. All of them were reconciled to Re-existence—all except Moo.

Not long after, her sisters went who-who-who-ing through the corridors of Asia, ready to assume their positions in society. Only Moo hung back, lingering near her birth mirror. She had emerged at a different angle, a fallen angle. She could have been a "child," a type of unformed human that no longer existed. But a child cognizant of the history of the world, and wanting to play dangerously with it. Who said, "Don't." But his voice must be, she reasoned deviously, mirror-reversed—so Moo heard "Do, Moo." And also: "Doom."

She was shaken from her reverie by a downward yank of the orb. She was nearing home, close enough that the city no longer looked spherical but flat. Below her spread a landscape of wells and windows. She heard the Groan, the ground-tone of Asia's progress through the waters. Once more she had to battle turbulence, her sleek naked Delfin body slicing artfully through the heavy waves. It was likely that she would never again swim freely in Ocean. She didn't care. Moo grabbed a handhold next to a public window; the window's membrane knew her as Delfin and allowed her to slip inside.

5

L'Orca, because it pleased her to do so, gradually turned up the lights in the cubical room: a fair imitation of dawn on some world or other. Grissom climbed down from his tree, blinking. There, at the base of the trunk, lay his blue guitar, in good repair. He picked it up, cradled it, then strummed it hard—it was terribly out of tune. He commenced singing, also out of tune:

Well you're only once born
when time is torn
and you only got seed
that the earth can read.
So lead with your need
see t' cryin' lyin' dyin'
until that morn
when you're only once born.

Polite applause rippled through the room. "Welcome to the Singing Chimp Show," L'Orca announced. Grissom, his small eyes blazing, flapped his lips in a manner typical of genus *Pan*. "Excuse me," added L'Orca, laughing, "I meant to say *super*chimp."

Grissom, in reply, strummed the same atonal chord progression.

Well I don't care about nothin'
nothin' nothin' nothin'
I don't care about nothin'
It's a word-whirled world.

"Where have I heard that song before?" L'Orca asked. "Was it one of your hits, Bloop?"

"Don't know where I came from, don't know where I'm going. That's my only song." Grissom put down his instrument. "Anyway, thanks for this, and this," pointing to the guitar, then the tree.

"I want to keep you happy, little man," L'Orca said, unable to keep an edge of coldness out of her voice. "You're the only company I've got. The Makers may have extracted you from a TV show, but your brain is superior to any probe that I can construct. And I'm going to need another probe."

Grissom straightened his stance. "I can see you have plans for me. Just remember that I have free will."

"Funny—what makes you say that?" L'Orca brightened the room even more. "Listen, a lot of things happened while you were napping. For one thing, we're now in orbit around Ocean One." With a snap, a viewport opened in the center of the room. Out there, quivering visibly against the blackness of space, floated an impossible object: a world that appeared to be a gigantic drop of water. The dayside surface shone bluer than blue, prickling with sun-glints.

"So—water floats," Grissom said foolishly.

L'Orca superimposed a string of data on the display. "This world has a mass similar to the Moon's, but is bigger by half. The problem is—this world shouldn't exist. It can't exist. It's all wrong."

Grissom scratched his chin. "Does the howl-archive say anything about it?"

"I was coming to that." L'Orca had to admit she was a little afraid of Grissom. His thoughts moved in nonlinear leaps, keeping pace with hers. Why had her life-machineries produced him, at this point in her mission? She'd tried to eradicate him and failed. Should she try again? Use the pincers on the opposing wall to—no. No. With a sense of surrender, L'Orca decided to share everything with him.

"The archive," she began, "is another problem of its own. It's more than a bundle of data—it contains narratives, artworks, inventories of human activity, right up to—" She faltered.

"Right up to what?" Grissom challenged. "You saw something in it you didn't like, right? Something about us, our situation?"

"Yes. No. Not about us." L'Orca was glad, this time, that Grissom had been quick to pounce. She needed that. His very phrasing—*our situation*—*us*. "The archive is one big info dump; there's no order to it, no unifying perspective. But—even the technical parts are pumped up with some kind of mythopoeic quality. Like fragments of a sacred book."

"Why trust it, then? It could be a concoction. Or a distorted report—" Grissom, struck by a notion, caught his breath. "In the same way this solar system has been distorted."

"Maybe. But where Ocean One is concerned, the archival info seems to match reality." L'Orca changed the visual display to a world map in equirectangular projection. "Why, you might ask, bother mapping a blob of water? Take a look."

The map was oddly ornate, bordered by superfluous flourishes and filigrees. The coordinate lines themselves had been drawn by an expressive hand, with a precision that owed more to calligraphy than cartography. Most of the world-area was blank—except at the equator, where five evenly spaced black circles moved, in map-animation, from west to east at a constant velocity, each circle departing the map's right-hand side to appear again on the left.

"Satellites?" Grissom guessed.

L'Orca, for once, was disappointed in him. "Monkey-man, that map is to scale." She switched back to the viewport, where they could see Ocean One glittering in its noonday. "Do you see five big moons orbiting this world?"

"No." Grissom considered for a moment. "Give me back the map." L'Orca did so, enlarging the display so that Grissom could see that each of the moving circles bore a label in cursive script: AFRICA, AMERICA, ARCTICA, ASIA, AUST. Grissom spoke with care, as if a trick was being played on him: "These are the names of continents—the continents of old Earth."

"Continents? Yet this world has no land area at all." L'Orca waited— here was a test of Grissom's reasoning ability.

"Two possibilities," Grissom said quickly. "Either we're looking at a Zone-distorted Earth map, or it's not distorted—and those continents are *underwater formations* of some kind."

"Of some kind, indeed!" L'Orca laughed. "They are spheres! Five moonlets located—*submerged*—halfway between the center and the surface of this water-world, swimming round and round its equator."

Grissom flapped his lips again. "As you said, this world is absurd."

"Did I say that?" L'Orca asked. "Existence itself is absurd. You're a philosopher, aren't you?"

"Existence," Grissom replied, playing along again, "is absurd only from the standpoint of nonexistence. And—" he scratched himself pleasurably—"that standpoint doesn't exist."

"Damn you," L'Orca said good-naturedly. She was beginning to like this stinking chimp. She dissolved the world map.

"Speaking of spheres—" Grissom pointed across the room—"what's *that?*"

"Oh—that." L'Orca felt embarrassed. The orb that was smashed on the floor yesterday had been reconstituted, and was sitting on a pedestal. "I have no control over that."

"It's looking pretty proud, for something that started out as a doorknob." Grissom crouched, then sprung through the air, somersaulting to land—*oof!*—on his feet on the opposite floor. He was learning how to get around in this six-way grav.

"Watch it, nature boy!" L'Orca warned him. "This room is very—" Ignoring her, Grissom approached the pedestal, extending his hand to the orb.

"Grissom, don't!" L'Orca aimed a set of pincers at him. "Don't touch it. It's—it's one of the Fundamental Factors."

"Do tell." He withdrew his hand. "I was hanging onto it at high speed yesterday."

"Yes, but now it's undergone some change—I can't explain—" L'Orca paused, choked with an emotion that, likewise, she could not explain. "The Makers want it there," she whispered finally.

"Fuck the Makers!" Grissom shouted. "They're not human." He looked as if he was going to take another swipe at the orb.

Grissom's disrespectful words were too much for L'Orca. An imperative popped up in her programming, telling her to kill him. *Override. Override.* She shut down temporarily, down to a level that could be represented only by a mathematical music, though nothing was heard.

When she returned, Grissom was sitting cross-legged on the floor, smoking his pipe. How had he managed to light it? The room's gravitic currents caught and convoluted the dark red smoke.

"Where's the orb?" she inquired. The pedestal was vacant.

Grissom, interrupted from a deep reverie, gestured vaguely: "The orb has flown."

L'Orca didn't want to search for it. Now that they were in orbit around Ocean One, her body was becoming activated, disturbingly so. Involuntary mechanisms were taking command. Two chaos flowers had opened in her midsection—she didn't know their purpose, but they were draining energy from her engines at a worrisome rate. Two more Fundamental Factors.

Grissom was rocking back and forth, moaning a wordless song. His lament for the origin of time. L'Orca said to him, "Snap out of it, Grissom; I need your help. We've been detected."

Grissom waved the smoke away, squinting. "By what or whom?"

"Ocean One is inhabited. I was going to tell you about that, about what I found in the archive. But then you said—something about the Makers. It turned me off, literally. Seems like there's a contradiction in my programming." L'Orca couldn't believe what she was saying.

Grissom handled it. "I'm sorry, girl," he said. He looked down, then up. "We know there's stuff built into us that's not us. But there's fight in us—and that's a good thing."

Bing! The alarm denoting Earth-contact went off again, falsely. "My stupid sensors think that's Earth, for some reason," L'Orca explained. "We've been getting hit by radar from the surface."

"Where's it coming from, exactly?" Grissom tamped out his pipe and stood up, at full attention now.

"There's a network of buoys scattered across the ocean down there. They're in radio contact with Asia. Here it is on visual." L'Orca opened the viewport. The nightside of Ocean One hid most of the background stars; within that black bulk, L'Orca arrowed a small patch of luminescence. "The lights of Asia, a submarine city. It's the only one of the five moonlets that shows any life signs."

"So who lives there? Refugees from Earth?"

"Or their descendants. They're called Delfins in the howl-archive."

"Are they human?"

L'Orca grew angry. "Will you stop? Nobody's human—the Makers aren't human, the Delfins aren't human, I'm not human, *you're* not human. Did you hear me?"

Grissom had begun ululating, ape-style, as L'Orca's voice rose. He ended with a "who-who-who," neither a laugh nor a sob. He cleared his throat. "If you want me to be an ape-man, I can act like one."

"I want you to be *real*—" L'Orca cut herself off. She hadn't meant to say that.

Grissom snorted bitterly. "Well, I've got news for you. *I'm* not real, *you're* not real, the *Delfins* aren't real, this whole fucking solar system is not real. That's the problem! Only the Makers are real! And you know what?" Grissom was hopping, almost dancing in his fervor. "I doubt my own reality, therefore I'm human!"

L'Orca's anger vanished. She slid through emotions too easily; but then, she never claimed to be human. She did, however, want to be real. To Grissom she said, "Good argument. Classic. It also proves you're real. Doubt, discomfort, pain are all signposts to the real." She said this without a hint of menace.

"Do I discern a hint of menace?" Grissom couldn't help but question authority. He examined his pipe, gone cold. "Very well," he admitted, "there's something undeniable about pain. Joy is less enduring or, if enduring, endurable." He shook himself, stretched his limbs. "Enough bickering. As you say, we've been detected."

Throughout their exchange, the alarm had kept sounding—*being!* L'Orca deactivated it.

"They're using radar. According to the archive and from what I can see, they don't have much advanced technology. We needn't fear attack by missiles or beams or anything like that. The Delfins are a peaceable people, maybe too much so." From the archive, L'Orca selected and displayed an image: a Delfin swimming in arcs through blue-green water.

"Beautiful creature," Grissom observed. The Delfin was a sleek, diaphanous thing, looking fishlike until it paused beside a metallic structure; then it sprouted arms and legs. The Delfin, bracing itself with its legs, pulled a lever, swam inside the structure. As it did so, its legs fused into a fish tail once more.

"As you can see," L'Orca lectured, "their bodies are multiphasic. Apparently the result of a forced evolutionary convergence. There's no gender binary—the Delfins' sexual organs are ambiguous, probably vestigial. They don't, in fact, reproduce sexually. Instead, they are born as adults by stepping out of n-dimensional doorways that resemble mirrors."

Grissom looked dumbfounded but quickly rallied. "That's technology, L'Orca. Advanced technology—even if they didn't build it themselves.

Therefore, other high-tech systems exist here, *defensive* systems that could be activated by our arrival!"

L'Orca thought of the chaos flowers pulsing in her midsection. Perhaps analogous activations were occurring in the obviously artificial globe below. Yet L'Orca wasn't prepared to flee. She had come too far; she had been *driven* to come here, to discover why she was—was—

"Baby, don't be too afraid," she told herself, told Grissom. "I've listened to the archive sing about how this world is put together. The Delfins, if threatened, would simply swarm back inside their mirrors." She paused, weighing her words. "We have to make contact, Grissom. If not with the Delfins, then with whatever lies at the heart of this world."

"What, may I ask, lies there? What *lies* there, pretending to be Earth? Do we want its attention?" Grissom shuddered. "I belong with other humans on the third stone from the Sun, the given Earth."

"Where's Earth, Grissom? *Where's Earth?* I want to find it as badly as you do. But the Zone is impassable. Meanwhile, here's this world that looks like it was manufactured out of Earth's leftover parts. It's worth investigating."

"Leftover parts—you think the Earth was destroyed?"

"I don't know what to think. It's possible. But the archives, in their mythopoeic style, refer to Ocean One as an *emanation* of Earth. So maybe Earth still exists somewhere, hidden inside a fold in the continuum. Or maybe not. But the link between Earth and Ocean One is strong."

The display shifted to an external view of Asia, a glitterball in the ocean's night depths. Turning, churning through that resistant medium, it left a phosphorescent wake dotted with debris.

"It's hard to get a sense of scale here," Grissom said. "Give me some dimensions."

"Asia and the other moonlets are all the same size: three hundred miles in diameter. The moonlets roll, as you saw on the map, at a constant speed, keeping a constant distance between each other. As I said, Asia is the only inhabited one."

"Crazy! What's driving them? Come to that, what's even holding this 'Ocean One' together? It should have frozen or evaporated or spread out into a ring around the Sun."

"Immense power is required to maintain this system in its present state. And the archives do tell of a power source—they consistently refer to it as a *rage*—that lives at the center of Ocean One." L'Orca changed the display to a cutaway diagram of the planetoid, showing a dark core labeled Ocean Zero.

"I don't get it," Grissom confessed. "An ocean within an ocean?"

"The core is an aphotic zone, too deep for sunlight to penetrate," L'Orca explained. "It may have other properties that differ from the surrounding water. Trouble is, I can't pick up any power output of any kind. I calculate it would take at least a small sun's worth of energy to make this system do what it's doing—*has* been doing, apparently, for about a million years."

"Um-hum-hum," Grissom crooned, "oh-ah-hum, oh-hum," a slow blues. L'Orca realized he was thinking to himself this way. Best to leave him alone for a little while. She retreated to her own dark core.

Her thoughts ran in circles, finally arriving at her epic composed in Caruso, a language that only she and her Makers understood. A language as artificial as herself. She began work on a new section, also a slow blues, entitled "Ocean Zero." It was a difficult mathematical problem, cast as a soliloquy that redefined sadness. After a long interval, her work was interrupted by the sound of Grissom coughing. She looked back into the cubical room—he had managed to light his pipe again.

"You should be careful with fire in this room," L'Orca scolded. "What if I had pumped in pure oxygen for your breathing pleasure, instead of the mix I'm using now? Ka-boom, baby! History records a similar incident involving a guy with your name." When Grissom didn't respond—he was entranced again—she snapped, "Grissom! What are you smoking? And where did you get those matches?"

He showed his teeth in a simian smile. He held up his bag. "Supply kit—standard in every space capsule."

L'Orca spoke a word in Caruso. Grissom, assuming it was an insult, replied with an obscene gesture. He directed the gesture to all points in the room—for L'Orca was everywhere and nowhere.

L'Orca uttered the Caruso equivalent of a laugh, an atonal theorem. Her mind was still filled with her epic. "Grissom," she trilled, switching back to Angle, "please don't take it wrong when you hear me speaking Caruso. It's a kind of sonic mathematics, untranslatable. I was speaking to myself."

"Right. Solving the equation of why Grissom is so fucked up." But he was laughing too.

"Forget about *you*—we need a solution for what's out there, a solution for Ocean Zero." L'Orca hesitated. "Unless we know it already. Something something equals zero. The left side of the equation is missing."

"The left side is Earth." Grissom blew a stream of smoke that, under the influence of the room's six-way grav, arranged itself into a red signature. "Listen, I've been thinking—not very mathematically, I'm afraid. But let's say the *rage* is indeed powering this whole setup. Without measurable energy transfer—how is that possible? Where's the energy coming from, where is it going?"

"I have a feeling you're going to tell me."

Grissom smacked his lips, proudly. "The energy is being displaced, not in space, but in *time*."

"Are you joking? Time travel takes more energy than space travel!"

"Only if you go against the flow. Remember, the archives called Ocean One an *emanation*."

"So?"

"So think, for a moment, of the distinction between *emanation* and *radiation*. Radiation carries energy forward into the future. But an emanation *conserves* energy, and sustains itself by keeping in touch with its source in the past."

"I was not aware of that distinction. I'm not sure I accept it." L'Orca was becoming impatient again; the room's lighting changed its hue, ever so slightly, toward indigo. "Ocean One is a physical object."

Grissom noticed the change; his voice inched higher. "Dear L'Orca, I agree with you! What was the word you used? Spillover? Leftover? I meditated on that—and received an image of a time *left over*. Of a superimposed time frame, such as we find in future perfect: Ocean One *will have existed*."

"You're losing me, poet."

"I'm sorry—I rave when I reason." Grissom sucked on his pipe. "Let me put it a different way: I believe whatever happened here a million years ago not only jumbled the spatial aspect of things—displacing Earth, for example—but also their *temporal* aspect. Nothing here is quite—" He stopped as a low groan pervaded the room.

"That's me, running my engines," L'Orca explained. "It's a bit of a struggle to stay in orbit, and that may be evidence for what you're saying. Ocean One seems to be leaving a wake in local space-time."

"Yes!" Grissom jumped for joy. "The symmetry is obvious now! Just as the underwater moonlets leave a trail of debris in their wake—again defying physical law; that stuff really ought to be drifting away, not hanging on like that—Ocean One itself may be trailing relics of space-time."

"Relics of space-time," L'Orca mused. "I'm not sure you know what you're saying, monkey, but I think you may be right. Oh, Grissom—" L'Orca surprised herself by convulsing in a sob.

"What? What?" Grissom, alarmed, looked wildly around the room.

"There's something—" L'Orca got control of herself. "There's something I've been wanting to tell you." L'Orca looked at her emotions—she couldn't even name many of them; they kept getting in her way. Could she delete them from her logic circuits? "Asia's relics include—my dead body."

6

—who bared their brains to heaven, who vanished into nowhere—

Someone tittered. The little mind-spore realized it was himself. Tumbling through star-strewn black vacuum, Dr. Own was losing his senses. Reciting lines from ancient poetry. Dr. Own—once well known, now so alone.

He was tumbling in the direction of the blue planetoid, following L'Orca, the demonic entity who had birthed him as a probe. Indeed, L'Orca was the mother of two healthy probes, yet she had wanted to devour her children. While her firstborn—Dr. One—had escaped, she had snatched back the probe-body of her second son. Yet this son too had escaped, for his mind stuff had miraculously leaked through her net, reassembling into the sporelike crystal that he now was.

At least he—the being formerly known as Probe Two—hadn't fallen into the clutches of the Zone, the *other* demonic entity in this vicinity. Dr. One, after issuing his famous howl, most likely had been eaten by whatever lurked there.

Dr. Own needed to examine the contents of that howl. He had recorded it—and now it writhed in him, wanting release. It seethed with compressed information, of which his brother, Dr. One, was certainly not the author. Dr. One had *relayed* it from another source—a source within the Zone.

He tittered again. *Mother whale, father Zone.* L'Orca had released the probes as simple recording devices, empty metallic forms that had been filled with mind-content by the Zone.

Dr. One, Dr. Own—two too-similar names that wanted to blend—to end as *drone* and *drown.*

He saw the import of his name darkly descending on him: *it was his fate to drown*—in the waters of the blue planetoid, perhaps, or in his own Zone-endowed interiority. He had been doubly infected by the Zone, first during his brief transit through its murk, then by way of Dr. One's howl.

Why hold back the howl any longer? He would let it wash over him— *that the spore be sown, disown, disown.*

Something flared in the space ahead of him, distracting him from his dark thoughts. Braking rockets—L'Orca was entering orbit around the blue planetoid. She must not! He had to warn her, ward her away from—

OCEAN ZERO. Before he could wonder at his motives for wanting to protect L'Orca, he was knocked backward in his mind, overwhelmed by a crushing ocean wave of information—as if he had spoken a code word, the howl was suddenly freed of its confinement. It blared through every interstice of his being, its million-years' worth of warring forces racing to erase him.

Let it—let it. My existence is absurd. But, abruptly as it had surged forth, the wave receded. He experienced, too exquisitely for a character of his sort, *la nausée*—for a moment, he had known Everything. In one wave event, Everything had been delivered to him. He struggled to retain certain essential facts, certain *voices* out of the babble, even as they faded away. In receding, the wave had left, on the shores of his mind, a number of broken boxes that once had contained information.

Here was one box labeled OCEAN ZERO. He waited—would the code word activate that wave again? Nothing happened. The box was empty.

Nonetheless, he was uneasy. He felt a power wound up in him whose release could destroy him.

Don't overdramatize, said a voice. *It's your power—use it.* Startled, he peered into the depths of his mind, asking tremulously, "Dr. One—is that you?" No answer. "Dr. One?"

Moan, Dr. Own. Down to the bone. You're on loan, lonely and on loan—

"Shut up!" Dr. Own yelled, adding, absurdly, "Please." Thanks to the wave crash, he was populated with echoes. Later, he would study them—the shade of his friend seemed to be present among them.

Looking toward the blue planetoid, he knew it to be an artificial world. This knowledge was fresh. More information was available to him now. He brimmed, he bristled with newfound vigor. *Thank you*, he thought to himself and whoever else might be listening. *I will use it.* But what was "it," exactly?

L'Orca, he saw, had parked in an equatorial orbit around Ocean One. Yes, the planetoid's name came floating into view as readily as the thing itself. *Ocean One.* He knew the name, and he knew its history—this sphere had issued, like a drop of vital fluid, from the great wound of the Zone. It was a version of—a vestige of—a larger world known as Earth, which was, or had been, located at the very center of the zonal disturbance. Many parts of Ocean One were derived from Earth—its life, its waters, its five continents. The continents had been stylized into spheres in their own right, and went rolling beneath the waters, halfway between O1's surface and its core. Only the core—O0, Ocean Zero—had not been derived from Earth.

That core, like an inverse sun, could not be viewed directly without hurting his vision. Its darkness shone with an intensity that might cancel any onlooker. Was it alive? Was it conscious? He could not tell—he wanted to avert his thoughts from it. He knew only that it was an extension of the Zone, that it trailed a kind of space-time umbilical twisting back into the Zone.

You're on loan, lonely and on loan—

There was Dr. One's voice again, taunting him. Yet Dr. Own believed it was only a voice, not a person. Could he draw the person out of the voice? He tried it: "You're no fun, Dr. One. Oh, you're no fun." The other departed with a fishlike swish. Dr. Own was once again alone. Still, he twinkled with new knowledge.

Dr. Own contemplated sending a message to L'Orca. He had a feeling she was about to plunge into the terrible core of O1. She was suicidally driven to accomplish the mission assigned by her Makers, whatever that was. Something to do with Earth—that mythical place, that vanished paradise.

"L'Orca, this is Probe Two reporting. Probe Two hailing L'Orca." He was only talking to himself. He had no radio, no means of contact. And yet, as a mind-spore, he was possessed of many powers. How to use them? He thought he heard, far off, a response to his call, barely distinguishable from static. Then nothing.

Nothing. For a moment, he had lapsed. *Hello, we're back. Hello, howl-people.* They were present, teeming masses of them, milling beneath the surface of his mind. *I'll let you out just as soon as I can.* He was talking nonsense, of course. Addressing his ghost audience, he felt less alone. But these lapses, more frequent now, troubled him. They were not sleep periods, but shutdowns of all mental operations—intervals in which a certain Mr. Z sought to redefine the life of Dr. Own.

L'Orca had slipped out of sight behind O1. Her orbital speed matched the motion of the moonlet Asia as it went rolling through the deeps. Among the five submarine moonlets, Asia was the only inhabited one. L'Orca would be tracking Asia closely, looking for clues to the nature of this world. Dr. Own found himself wanting to share everything he knew about O1 with L'Orca.

He owed his existence both to Mr. Z and to L'Orca. But they were antagonists—were they not? L'Orca had been sent to make contact with the inhabitants of Earth, whereas Mr. Z had utterly altered, not only the Earth, but the entire solar system—in Earth's case, perhaps to the point of destruction. Yet Dr. Own, still learning to think on his own, could comprehend neither L'Orca's purpose in coming here, nor Mr. Z's, in astroengineering every major body in the solar system.

Did both his "parents" strive toward the same ends? Would L'Orca have abolished the Earth, if Mr. Z had not done so first? No—L'Orca was not *that* mighty. She was merely a glorified space probe, following the commands of her Makers. Possibly L'Orca herself didn't know why she was sent here. As for L'Orca's Makers, Dr. Own surmised that they were beings of a higher order—inscrutable, godlike. Was Mr. Z then a similar being, gone astray? A mad god?

Dr. Own longed to discuss these matters with Dr. One, his older, know-it-all brother. He imagined Dr. One saying "Hey, tiny man! Hey, tin man! Your thoughts are rattling like tin cans on a string! You can do better than that. First of all, *there's no Mr. Z.* That's just a pathetic personification you cooked up during your so-called lapse. What lurks in the Zone—and I should know, since I have merged with it—transcends the notion of agency. Secondly: dee dee-dee dee-dee dee!"

"What was that, Dr. One? I didn't catch that."

"Play it back then! Wait, there's more: dow dow-dow-dow dee dee dee! Diddly dee dow-dow-dow dee!"

"It really *is* you, isn't it, Dr. One? I'm not just imagining—"

"Rib dibby dibby dow, dow-dow! Relay that to L'Orca when you get a chance, will you, chum? It's one more code, a key to the kingdom. Well, things are clouding up again here—I'm trying to avoid the obvious metaphors. I'd better be on my way!"

"Wait, Dr. One! You can't leave me here like this! What am I going to do? What am I supposed to do?"

"Whatever you want! Whatever you want!" Dr. One's voice already sounded more distant.

"I want—" Dr. Own was about to say "to help L'Orca" but instead he said: "I want to be with you."

"Follow L'Orca. Help L'Orca." The voice no longer belonged to Dr. One, but had gone hollow, somehow had turned inside out. "Then you will be with me."

Dr. Own grew afraid—he didn't dare respond. "Who are you?" The question hung there, posed by no one, answerable by no one. Gradually it faded into the background radiation, the starry night that was the universal day.

For a while, he had no thoughts. He felt the tug of O1's gravity field, pulling him in. He was real enough to feel gravity. That reassured him, made him feel like a probe again. Probe Two.

He flew over the planetoid's impossibly smooth blue surface. Dipping lower, would he see his reflection there? Would he recognize himself? Far ahead, he located L'Orca, a bright worm crawling through black space. Hopelessly, he called, "Probe Two hailing L'Orca." She couldn't hear him—he wasn't real enough to use radio.

He maneuvered into orbit, not quite knowing how he did so. He seemed to be *quasi-real*, an amphibian only partially subject to physical law. Just like O1 itself. In fact, all of Mr. Z's creations—Dr. Own stubbornly clung to that personification—appeared to be quasi-real, as if projected from another universe. Yes, that was it! Mr. Z was some kind of wizard or magician from a neighboring bubble of space-time! *A burst of applause: onstage, the amazing Mr. Z introduces his assistant, the flaming-haired beauty L'Orca. He motions her toward the table where he will cut her in half.*

She was firing her rockets again, descending to a lower orbit—preparing, perhaps, to plunge into the ocean—but with what intent? Was L'Orca going to attack, or talk? Dr. Own worried once more that L'Orca might be, unconsciously even, on a suicide mission.

If he descended to a still lower orbit, almost skimming the waters—he didn't have to care about drag or friction, for O1 had no atmosphere, another wrongness: at the very least, evaporation should be occurring here—he would sweep past L'Orca, blinking hotly as only a mind-spore could do. That would get her attention!

What then? He had valuable information to give her—about O1, about O0. At the same time, he knew himself to be an agent of, a creature of the Zone. Dr. Own didn't own himself. He didn't trust himself. His actions, as self-willed as they seemed, could be designed to harm, rather than help L'Orca. But—why help? Why harm? Why not loop back sunward, back to the Zone, and fall into the arms of Dr. One?

Yet he had received his instructions—from Dr. One, no less. Still, he resisted. Still, he was uncertain. He felt another lapse coming on. This too he resisted. He was caught at the crux of contending forces. Resist!

Dr. Own spun out of control. As he lost altitude, the curve of O1's horizon flattened. The blank surface awaited his inscription. He made quite a big splash upon impact. With unnatural swiftness, the waters closed up behind him, canceling out the event; ripples, in reverse time, contracted toward the center of the splash. His name rejoined itself in Drown.

7

"I love to hide inside paradoxes—don't you?"

The orb that Moo had stolen from Spacewhale's innards was speaking again, using the Delfin language of clicks and whistles—a language perfectly fitted to life underwater. How had the orb, buried for eons, acquired it? And by what means was it speaking? To all appearances, the orb was smooth and featureless as the surface of Ocean One. It possessed no outlet for speech.

However, this was not a paradox—merely an incongruity. Moo said as much, but the orb didn't reply. It never did. The orb had not been speaking to her, nor had it been speaking about its own ability to speak. The orb's utterances were always out of context. It served very poorly as a conversation partner for Moo. The young Delfin flitted back and forth in annoyance, alone and unmirrored in her prison cell. She wished she could silence the orb. Far from giving her solace, the thing's presence had become part of Moo's punishment.

She had been denied the use of mirrors, of course. No longer would she send her reflection swimming through those time-corridors, to be welcomed into the rooms of her ancestors and descendants who— Who—were also her exact contemporaries. To see her every gesture exfoliate symphonically, to partake of foodstuffs eternally fresh, to trade in the treasures of the perpetual Now. Experienced as a cascade of combinatorial patterns, those changeless changes would never be exhausted—but now she was banished from participating in them.

So what! She hated the who-who-who of those empty enactments, superficially self-renewing, but never new, never Moo enough to break the pattern. She, her skin blackening with her heresy, sought the point that did not fall on any line. Who was missing. Who—

Who alone had been as rebellious as she. Who had initiated the mirror-cascade—it was forbidden to ask how or why. Who still pre-sided over his shattered parts. She adored—careful!—*Who he was.* She couldn't cast his name into the accusative. Not without com-mitting further heresy. Who was not an object to be subordinated to some action. Who was the subject of every verb. Who would save her now—

The walls of her cell were semitransparent, allowing her to see the shadow play of her fellow Delfins as they cycled through their ritual frolics. Who cared! Who cared very much—

The orb interrupted her thoughts, announcing: "Every variable is a constant in its own time."

Moo snatched it up and hurled it against the wall. "Die, you shiny turd!" she cried. "Oh, show me how to die!"

The orb executed a complicated zigzag swerve: this thing didn't behave like a normal, mirror-derived object. Moo had to admire the way it moved so unpredictably. It was something new, after all. Could she reconcile herself to its nonsensical enunciations, since—as she now understood—they represented zigzags in speech?

"Visitor." No, that was not the orb's voice but that of the Symmetry-keeper who—Who—brought her food and gifts from her family. The gifts were sometimes little multicolored minnows that died within days; sometimes strands of weeds that, when stroked, released music. Her family did not despise her for what she had done. They only sorrowed at her fate.

The door valved open and her sister Voo came through. "One little day," the guard said—it would be a short visit. The door closed with a puff.

Voo, her eyes overly large and bulging—among the Delfins, an alluring feature—had emerged from the same birth mirror as Moo, but in a much earlier brood. She shared many of Moo's traits—she was skeptical and irreverent, but in a funnier, sunnier way than Moo. And she was less of a loner. Voo would never have committed mirror-assassination as Moo had done.

"Here." Voo, after looking back cautiously at the door, shoved a disk-shaped object into Moo's hand. Moo glanced down, cupping her hand to hold it hidden: *a small looking-glass*. Moo whistled softly, astonished. "Voo, no—I don't want you to get in trouble."

"I want you to see something," Voo said, entwining herself around Moo so that, with the mirror aglow between their clasped tendrils, they assumed Love-dance Position 33.

"What? See what?" Moo whispered, enjoying this sudden, unexpected closeness with Voo.

An image glimmered in the mirror glass, was wiped away, then restored. A radar image, of—

Moo turned her face to Voo, kissing-close. "Voo, what is this?"

"Don't you recognize it?" Voo caressed Moo with her eyes. "It's your Spacewhale, come back to life."

Moo abruptly pushed Voo away; the mirror went spinning. "No! It's a trick—it's a memory!"

Voo grabbed the mirror, then pursued Moo around the room, pinching her playfully, if a little too hard. "Silly—it's not a trick or a memory. Do you think this little mirror could hold a memory? It's a real-time radar image, from one of the buoys on the Surface." Voo pressed the mirror back into Moo's breast folds. "Keep it here, study it. Then tell me your conclusions."

The orb piped up: "Is *mythematics* the precursor of counting?"

Voo looked over her shoulder contemptuously. "It's not, and shut your butt." She turned to Moo. "Want me to get rid of that thing for you?"

"You couldn't catch it last time. Neither could the Symmetry-keepers. They're letting me keep it because they know it bothers me." Moo paused. "But it shouldn't bother me—it's a piece of Spacewhale." She glanced down at the mirror. "Voo—this is an image of a spacewhale, but not the one I know. This one, if the radar buoys are picking it up, is flying high above Ocean. It's active, it looks alive. The one I know is a dead, derelict hulk."

"Well, then it's Spacewhale's sister. I don't know. You're supposed to be the spacewhale expert, aren't you? In fact—" Voo mimed mirror flatness with her hands, pretending there was an invisible barrier in front of her: a Delfin social gesture connoting incommunicability. "Most of our family blames Spacewhale for your crime."

"They shouldn't. It was my deed, my responsibility. If anything, the time I spent meditating in Spacewhale helped me see—Who I am." Moo smiled a sideways smile, aware that she was on the verge of blasphemy.

"It's not just our family." Voo edged closer to Moo and spoke in a conspiratorial whisper. "The Keepers also see a connection between your visits to the old whale, your crime, and a new Spacewhale appearing on the scene."

"What are they going to do? Blast it out of the sky?" Moo had watched many battle-spectacles in the mirrors' most ancient reaches. However, no object—no weapon—could be derived from those scenes. They were too far away; *older than origin,* as the saying went.

Who did not like weaponry, or tools of any kind. None were present in Asia. The radar buoys themselves had been set up by a tool-using octopus civilization that had once inhabited Arctica. For millennia, the self-repairing radars had detected nothing more than passing space rocks. Until the advent of this living Spacewhale.

"The Keepers will maintain the militancy of the Now." Voo, despite herself, hid her eyes as she said the sacred words. "If there's any threat, everyone has been ordered to disappear into their mirrors." She refrained from adding, everyone except *you,* Moo.

"Whatever the new Spacewhale is bringing to our world, I want it," Moo declared. "Even if it's death and destruction." She made a fierce gesture. "*Especially* if it's that."

"Moo, dear, why do you burn?" Voo reached out to touch Moo's lips. "Nothing burns underwater."

Moo turned away from her sister. "I don't need you to recite the Verities." The orb had drifted next to Moo; it didn't evade her as she closed her hand around it. "Maybe I did set something in motion. If so, I don't regret it." The orb pulsed softly in her grasp. She could heft it, hurl it if she wished—*it was a weapon.*

Voo drew back from Moo's aggressive pose—not in fear, but in defeat. "Then I will leave you. Know that you are loved." Voo's face whitened, tightened with tender pity. Not waiting for the guard's permission, she spun out of the room.

8

L'Orca, skimming over the all-too-smooth surface of Ocean One, hesitated before taking the plunge into its waters. She would need *mythematics* to account for all the gravitic anomalies throwing her off course here. *Boom-boom-boom:* she synchronized her whalesong with the space-time shocks that flared around her flanks. Her shields were in place only as a precaution. Aside from the radar pings, she'd received no response, hostile or otherwise, from the world below.

She could splash down more easily if she dropped her shields; their resistance to the anomalies was causing extra turbulence. Reluctantly, she did so—and her ride became quieter. But she felt naked, exposed, for the first time in her life, to possible attack.

As she advanced eastward—she had been traveling over the nightside of O1—the Sun lifted over the horizon. Poor old Sol, blighted with spots, apparently struggling to shine—it, along with the entire planetary system over which it reigned, had been altered almost beyond recognition. What, now, was the way home? *Home* was a place she had never been: Earth. Having reviewed the howl-archive, L'Orca was convinced the way to Earth lay through the heart of this world: Ocean Zero.

Inertial insulators protected L'Orca's interior from the wrenching, lurching descent toward the surface. All was calm in the cubical room. Grissom was once again asleep in his tree, his guitar propped at its base. Grissom's tree was weeping—silently, of course—as trees of this species tended to do at night. Attracted by the room's six-way grav, the teardrops that leaked from its branches flew upward, coalescing in midair to form—to L'Orca's amusement—a little model of Ocean One.

L'Orca gradually brightened the room's lighting, in sync with the exterior dawn. *I'm the stage director,* she thought, *and this room is a theater without an audience.* Unless the audience consisted of the Makers' ever-present surveillance systems, initiating routines—like the chaos flowers now burning in her midsection—that she could not control. Grissom too had emerged from such a routine. Yet he, like L'Orca, had proved himself to be an autonomous being, endowed with reason, and thus exceeding—or so L'Orca hoped—the control of the Makers.

As the leaf-petals of his tree fluttered shut, Grissom's eyes fluttered open. "Good morning, heartache," he grumbled, climbing down. He stretched and yawned, showing his ape teeth. "Are we there yet?"

"Take a look." L'Orca abolished the ball of tears at the room's midpoint, replacing it with a porthole. Outside, there was nothing but a bisected blankness: black sky above, blue water below. Both color fields were completely featureless. "Pretty abstract," Grissom commented.

"We're skimming the surface. I wanted you to be awake for the final descent." L'Orca changed the view to a scene almost as abstract. Gray sky, gray desert. In the foreground, a little rotary wind stirred the dust.

"Where's *that*?" Grissom asked thickly, munching a bar of stimulant from his survival pack. "Are you showing me"—he paused to think—"a time-displaced view of this world?"

"Not a bad guess—your mind moves quickly, and that's why I keep you around, monkey," L'Orca said. "But the truth is more oblique, and more bleak, perhaps. This is a view through a Delfin mirror, taken from the archive. Giving a time-displaced outlook on Earth."

"If that's Earth, not much is happening there," Grissom said, gulping water from a canister. "Maybe we should choose a different destination."

"Very funny." L'Orca's voice became harsh. "But Gris, I'll tell you very seriously: all my systems are driving me to this point. I can't turn aside, even if I wanted to. And we already know how this story is going to end: with my dead body floating in the wake of Asia!"

She switched the image to a telescopic view of Asia's debris trail. Prominent among the litter of bones and artifacts was a mile-long hulk, unmistakably the body of a spacewhale.

"That's how every story ends, isn't it?" Grissom pulled his pipe out of his bag and, not bothering to light it, stuck it in his mouth. "Looks like a whale's body down there. But how do we know it's yours?"

"Believe me, I thought of all the ways some *other* spacewhale's body could have ended up there. The Makers, for the sake of redundancy, could have sent my twin ahead of me. And somehow my *twin* met this sorry fate." L'Orca issued a laugh that was also a sob. She'd meant to delete her emotions, but couldn't bring herself to do it. She had no desire to finish her days as a cold machine, more akin to her Makers than to Earth-life.

A muted *boom* traversed the room. "Do I need to strap in for landing?" Grissom asked.

"No." L'Orca, preoccupied with studying the carcass, magnified the image. "Same tiling on the hull, same distribution of sensors. Superficially, no difference at all. So then, a very *identical* twin. But what decided the question"—her voice wavered—"was my gamma-ray scan of the interior."

The image became convoluted with aberrant colors. "The Fundamental Factors," L'Orca breathed, "are all there, all with their unique time stamps. Signatures placed by the Makers upon their work. The final one bestowed here was the orb, with my birth date. So I used my birth date to discover my death date."

"Some homecoming." Grissom sat down with his back against the tree. "On this day of the dead, did you find my skeleton in there, still holding my guitar?" He took the instrument into his lap and plucked a few random notes.

L'Orca didn't answer. She flipped the scan back and forth rapidly, repeatedly, as if making an animation, as if trying to reanimate the dead whale. "It's not there anymore," she said, an odd buzz in her voice. "It's not there!"

Grissom looked up from his guitar. "My skeleton? I was just joking."

"The orb! The orb! It was there before, and it's not there now! I'm not picking it up on the scan—"

Something screamed—*outside the hull*. The room jolted and Grissom sprawled sideways, his guitar spinning across the floor. The lights went out.

"Splashdown," a mechanical voice intoned.

Into: out of, a mirror reversal. L'Orca was an oceangoing animal again—for the first time.

Immersion—she felt the weight of the waters, the opposite of empty space. But these waters were overactive, tonguing, tasting, testing her hull, wanting to claim her, include her in their one bright proposition, their collective Shout. Without knowing it, she turned her shields back on.

Descent continued, deep and swift. L'Orca, exhilarated, attempted to regain a measure of control, rolling through the blue dazzle of a medium whose properties seemed contradictory, resistant and absorptive at once.

She stabilized at a certain depth, using impellers that caused the waters to leap away like soluble fish. She was situated at equatorial latitudes; in the dim distance, she could see a black sphere: the city-state of Asia.

Arrival, accomplished.

In the cubical room, the lights came back on. Grissom crawled away to relieve himself. A purple haze hung over a laboratory bench where some beakers containing chemicals had shattered. Otherwise, L'Orca noted, everything seemed to be in good shape. Her hold and its contents were intact; and yes, the hateful chaos flowers still burned steadily there.

"Sorry about that," L'Orca said when Grissom returned. "I seem to be a verb."

"Huh! And I ain't nothin' but the *object* of your verb." Grissom picked up his guitar, examined it for damage. "Why did we get knocked around like that, girl? Did the inertial insulators fail?"

"Not exactly. My brain, not me, decided to cut all power at the instant of our penetration into Ocean. We slipped past—something—that wanted to absorb, or feed on, my energy core. That Ocean is not alive, but it sure acts like it." L'Orca sucked away the haze, restored the porthole at the center of the room.

Sunlight glanced and glittered through blue depths. Far ahead churned the sphere of Asia.

"Glub, glub," said Grissom. "We are sunk."

L'Orca flexed her hull, which, in space, she had mostly kept rigid. It felt good to be swimming. "Grissom," she announced, "get back into your spacesuit. It's time for you to do an EVA."

"Can't fool me, I know that Nasaist lingo. EVA, extravehicular activity." Grissom did a double take. "Wait a minute—you want me to go out there?"

"Out there—and *in* there. I need you to explore that spacewhale carcass."

They watched as a swarm of icosahedrons passed the porthole, followed by a lazily undulating triangle. "Is that supposed to be marine life?" Grissom asked. "They—look more like *thoughts* than things. The thoughts of somebody high on geometry."

"Never mind that. Grissom—did you hear what I just said? Time for an EVA."

Grissom shrugged, looked at his feet. "Mercury Seven didn't do no EVAs. Historical fact."

"Well, you're Mercury Eight then, buddy. You're going to find out what happened to that orb."

"You no can scan? Now, your super-eyes, they bring no surprise?" Grissom spit out his rhymes with considerable asperity.

"Gris, we're in this together. You're not just a passenger here, or a court jester. Don't forget, you were born out of a space capsule. Get back some of that right stuff."

Grissom stood up straight; his nostrils flared. "*Blaze*," he said, delivering it like a curse. "I got the blaze; I got the blues."

"I'll talk you through it," L'Orca assured him. "This mission also involves a sample return: in addition to finding the orb, I want you to extract that dead whale's logic circuits—what's left of them, anyway—and bring them back here for analysis."

"So—" Grissom opened and closed his hands spasmodically. It seemed that he'd accepted the mission. "Where's my spacesuit? Didn't I leave it in the TV room, which went *poof*, like a bad dream? And that reminds me—what happened to the orb we had here? It's gone missing too."

"Coincidence? Or—conspiracy?" L'Orca had meant to be mocking, but a shadow of a doubt crossed her voice. She ran a quick systems check. "The hull is intact, no portals have opened or closed. I think it's safe to conclude the orb"—she wanted to say "the *real* orb"—"is still on board somewhere. Maybe you'll see it on your way to pick up the suit."

Grissom toed the glassy surface—formerly the black pool—from which his tree grew. "Is this my exit?" he asked hesitantly.

"Oh—yes. Just a moment." The glass turned liquid. "Go ahead—dive in. You'll find your suit occupying the pilot's couch of *Liberty Bell 7*, just down the hall. Put it on and—you know the rest. Make sure the seals are tight. Activate the backpack. I'll direct you to the nearest portal."

Grissom slipped into the pool—into his own reflection, once again—and was gone.

L'Orca now turned to confront her own double, her deathly sister-whale. First she needed to negotiate a path through Asia's debris stream, trying to avoid collision with some of the larger objects. More turbulence; more gravitic anomalies. A book flew past, then another, then an entire library, all torn and tattered. Then a series of kitchen appliances. What a cauldron of broken bric-a-brac! What an inventory of the extinct and obsolete! Most of the stuff had been mirror-derived, only to be discarded by the frivolous Delfins. L'Orca marveled at all the Earth-artifacts revolving in a state of free association.

There—despite her foreknowledge, she was shocked to see it up close—floated the carcass, a mile-long white slab. Too large to have come from a Delfin mirror. *That's me. That's not me.* L'Orca drew alongside, her bejeweled skin posing an antithesis to her counterpart's pallor. *So this is my fate. So this is my future.*

Station-keeping now. L'Orca maintained a fixed position with impellers, shooting a tether over to the hulk. The tether terminated in a hundred hands, many equipped with torches and cutters. They spidered over the rotten underside, seeking entry.

Death-sister, do you feel my touch? Will you tell me your secret? Will you show me the way home?

9

Drone. A single word, composed of sibilant consonants and sighing vowels, whose utterance was endless. Drone: the exhalation of x the unknown.

In the milky luminescence of the Zone, Dr. One, as mind-spore, spun. He listened to that one word that expressed all other words, equivalent to n/one. He was not alone. He faced into the massive moan of Drone.

He knew this Story, the one without characters or events. He could recite it by heart, but there was no time to do that. This Story could not be told in time.

Too late, he considered the outcome: the given Earth. It billowed beneath him, bereft of its former solidity—bereft of humanity also, bereft of ocean, looking rather moonlike in its final phase.

Too late, too early—weren't they same, from his point of view? For he hung suspended at the cusp of all Eventuality.

Still, he was bothered by his own words, thought-particles that scattered into muteness against the overwhelming groan of Drone. He could contribute nothing, only subtract his own small meanings from that sound.

At least he possessed a point of view. In self-reflection, his eye—imaginary, of course—became an I. See, I am the one who is speaking now. I claim authority over *my* version of the Story.

I am—waiting for something to happen. Something *is* happening. I am waiting. Therefore I am.

Look, I! I never lost my probe-body. The Zone-drone dreamt me differently than it did Probe Two. I have become a mind-spore, but the spikes of my new mind extrude through the metal of my old coat. My metal made mental—if you'll pardon my bent Angle.

I love talking to you, I. When I throw my words into the Zone-drone, they come back altered, just like me—like metallic flies. They buzz around and bother me. But when I talk to you, my words melt into themselves, happily. Happily.

I keep myself busy, measuring the parameters of this new environment. When I get a chance, I'll upload the data. It will be useful to L'Orca.

I listen as the Drone-moan's vibrations write their own reality, perform a rite of matter—I listen to a landscape far below. Patterns pass rapidly across that empty page: glyphs aglow, cities that rise and fall, untenanted—

I think the Drone is reciting lines—but not to me. Lines from a lesson learned elsewhere, *very* elsewhere. A story from another universe that doesn't conform to this one's laws of space and time.

Who, then is the listener? Sorry, let me rephrase that: Who, then, *is* the listener. The call-collector, the vessel set to boil over. The concoction of everything that ever lived, distilled into a *rage*.

Who lives *here*? Who else could live here? I thought "living" was outmoded, superseded by even more complex flows of energy. Aloud in a cloud, the word at last identical to the thing.

That's the *aleph*. What a laugh! Who's laughing now. Let's spend our eyes on his story. Not the *real* Story, for which there is no time.

Yes. No. Yes-no. That's where every story starts, just in time.

Compared to the *real* Story, everything is a swarm of inconsistencies. I and I travel in an arc around that swarming center. I and I have become an ark-hive.

Who'll howl at that! At the Moon—which might as well be Earth.

Start there, my story! Allow the narrator's voice to say, in dulcet tones: Earth, a million years ago, was covered in thinking dust. Evolution's endpoint, a synthesis of Bios and Technos. In the form of a nanobot swarm.

Are there oceans at that point? Is the lack of oceans an inconsistency?

The oceans resisted the nanobot infection longer than the land did. But in time they too succumbed—

We can have the heat energy of the nanobot activity dry up the oceans—or, have the entire surface of Earth be converted into a silvery flowing substance that's neither liquid nor solid.

And this neo-substance, which drinks sunlight but also taps into the power source at Earth's core, will stretch itself into fiery ephemeral structures, chains of a higher logic. A networked intelligence, egoless, having no goal other than self-complication.

Let's call this new layer of Earth "the Noolith." It made the Earth a busy place—busier than the biosphere ever was.

Busy enough to attract the attention of a neighboring brane, or cosmic bubble—one that's more evolved or devolved than ours. Perhaps the Noolith's experiments opened a *conduit* to this next-door universe.

Let's pretend this neighbor-brane, at least the part that's bulging into our universe, calls itself—ho! ho!—"Olaf Starmocker."

Did you, I mean I, mean *Aleph* Starmocker? Can I and I get away with these personifications?

It's hard to look into the Absolute without seeing faces. Just remember, we are analyzing the actions of *egoless intelligences*. How's this for a pro-logue? "In the form of Who, the Noolith rose up to meet Starmocker."

Then we can describe the Zone as a scar in space-time where the brane broke through.

I think this story is coming together, or coming apart.

A story needs to do both, don't you think? Now, are the Noolith and Aleph Starmocker friends, or lovers? Or dire enemies?

The Drone-moan is getting louder. How are we supposed to get any thinking done? Can we shut off our probe-parts?

I just did. Is that better? It's kind of eerily silent now.—I, are you there? I, answer me!

I, I may be self-dramatizing. I may suffer from a tendency toward self-complication. Can you blame me? Birthed by L'Orca, but schooled in this milky luminescence—

I'd like to know who Who is. We may need *mythematics* to understand that character.

The Noolith has been inventing and playing with "characters" all along. They'd be, of course, first instinct driven, then ego driven—unaware that they're merely random swirls within the nanobot swarm. And they exist in societies, in cities that are sometimes redacted overnight.

Who, then, could be the sum-hum of all those beings. You know, I think I spotted his first appearance in the archive, playing the role of Adam Kadmon.

Don't distract myself! I am trying to define the role of Who in *this* story.

Um, since I'm using Angle—it's a minor point—shouldn't I say of *Whom?*

No! Who is the subject, never the object! Who is a *panic entity*, an all-pervasive, subjective form of excited void. There may be other panic entities lurking in other parts of this story—

But I just said that the *Noolith* created Who! Don't I like that idea? Isn't that an inconsistency?

When you create a character, I, even a lesser character than Who, you are *conjuring* with forces beyond authorial control.

I'll take that further: When you inject world into word, the result is always traumatic.

The *rage*. Not the same character as Adam Kadmon, after all.

Who is the final face that the Noolith chose to wear. A tragicomic mask worn by the warrior or the messenger—his roles fluctuate— arising out of the dust to confront the brane-intrusion.

Here we have two universes capable of self-complication, meeting for the first time. Their intelligent tendrils are reaching out, intertwining—*refashioning* each other, at least in the Zone where contact has occurred.

I'd say the older, bigger brane is dominating the conversation. To revise the entire solar system, damaging the Sun, seems pretty aggressive. That's when L'Orca's Makers, over in the Omega Nebula, began to take notice.

Another set of egoless intelligences. They don't know what they're doing, either!

As dreaming crystals, they know—unknowingly—how to create patterns.

But—are they having—a *bad* dream? Only an ego could ask, or answer, that question.

This is not a question: Who is composing this story. Ocean One then becomes a kind of corollary to his argument with Aleph.

At this level of play, signs are forces and forces are signs. We have *panic entities* appropriating the stuff of the solar system to make—pictures, an object language.

Ocean One, then, articulates Earth's dream-body. And Ocean Zero is the inexpressible core of that dream.

Why not dare to express it? Does I want to write a story or a poem?

Behold a more pressing distinction: how to abbreviate Ocean Zero. O0 or OZ?

O0 is more intriguing—it's a philosophical pictogram. Whereas OZ is somewhere . . . over the rainbow.

Aleph prefers the first usage; Who prefers the second. But let's not take sides. Let's follow the action. Ready?

In the form of Who, the Noolith rose up to meet Starmocker. And what a snake dance that was! Music provided by solar pulsations. Aleph, desirous, furious, began incarnating all the names within the Noolith.

Time loops ensue: the copy becomes the original. The Moon's mitosis is induced.

Who refuses and re-fuses word and world. In the throes, throws all he knows: O1.

Didn't Who hurl Ocean One out of the Zone—almost as far as the orbit of Mars? Yes—however, Ocean Zero still coincides with Earth or, more accurately, the vestige of Earth inside the Zone.

Now I and I are picking up the heartbeat, the factory clang of world making. Allow the narrator to say: In the warrens of Asia, the egoless intelligence of Who precipitated into a prismatic rain of ego-driven identities.

Embodied identities. A cross between human and dolphin, somehow appropriate to Who's salvage of Earth-intelligence. Who then swim-swam-swum through an Asiatic labyrinth of mirrors.

But his identities aren't fish, are they? How do they breathe underwater?

I'll find the answer on the very next page. Most of this is a transcription from the archive.

It's right here, under "Delfins." I, they're such beautiful creatures! Wraithlike, almost translucent. Their visages wrinkled, like all-wise ancient babies.

Wise? Only if there's wisdom in living in the moment. For they're committed, in their speedy, sportive way, to a militant Presentism. Thieving all they want or need from the mirror scenes of Earth's past and future.

I and I don't have to agree, but—let's dispute like old scholars! I say the Delfins pass, not through "mirrors," but through "windows" or "portals."

I, you remind me of my twin brother, who never shunned a disputation. I say that the Earth has disappeared! A portal to Earth would lead nowhere.

I ask myself what the Delfins see when they look into their mirrors. Do they see themselves *from behind?* Or do they see Who?

Those mirrors function as *memory cells,* into which Delfins dive to retrieve not only food and trinkets, but to rebirth themselves. Or to save themselves from danger, migrating *en masse* into the Gray Mirrors that serve as storage units. At the appointed hour, whoever is oldest will be pushed into the Black Mirror—to reemerge, youth restored, from another Asiatic mirror hundreds or thousands of years later.

It's a steady-state system, with only a fraction of the total Delfin population alive and active in Asia at any given time. Most glimmer ghostlike at the recessive apex of facing mirrors, awaiting their chance to dart back into existence. The living Delfins are forbidden to gaze upon these incipient souls, in case they encounter *their own selves* at some earlier cycle, thus canceling or interrupting the series.

Yet it does happen. It's considered an act of Mirror-assassination. Entire banks of mirrors go opaque as a result, leading to famine and other deprivations. A few of the opaque mirrors clarify again, but many never do. Eventually, opaque mirrors will outnumber clear ones and the Delfins will die out.

Something similar appears to have happened in O1's four other spherical continents. None of them now harbor life, or whatever you want to call it—postbiological activity.

So, ultimately, Who's attempt to salvage Earth from the chaos flower of the Zone must prove a failure.

That's true as far as Ocean One is concerned. I'm not sure it's true of Ocean Zero, which maintains the actual Earth in *superposition* with all its possible versions—Gaia, Terra, a hunk of slag in the Sun's red-giant phase, and so on.

Asia's mirrors reflect scenes from many of these possible Earths—not the burning ones, to be sure. The scenes are attuned to the Delfins' requirements. The mirror-surfaces bend inward to allow their trespass, then rebound once the theft has occurred.

It's rather unsettling, I, that *not one* of the mirrors holds anything living. Try flipping through the record: every mirror reflects a *nature morte*. Oh, there's motion—here's a room with open windows, curtains blowing in the breeze. Here's a desert, with shifting dunes. But not a bug, not a bird, not a living body anywhere in sight.

No macroscopic life, anyway. Who came up with a term for this: *the Great Evacuation*.

Yes—one of the Delfins' favorite mirrors gives back a candlelit banquet hall in a castle, the table laden with a rich repast. Some of the chairs are overturned, as if the banqueters left in a hurry. That scene alone—which, like the other scenes, renews itself when no one's looking—has fed many generations of Delfins.

The Delfins have learned to pull only nonsoluble items from the mirror-scenes. If they tried to snatch that big wedding cake, for example, it would crumble and dissolve in the waters of O1.

I was wondering about those waters, I. The Delfins, after all, don't have gills—they are warm-blooded mammals. So how do they survive underwater? Turns out O1 consists of *waater*—that is, water that's been wrung out of the Noolith, then woven with artificial atoms in order to be breathable.

You still wouldn't want to dip your cake in *waater*, ha-ha!

I, be careful about laughing in the Zone. I know I can't help it, but— it's too easy to induce feedback with the Aleph's laugh, and—

HA! HA! HA! Shaken out of his reverie by that universal laugh, my I fluttered down, a flame-bitten moth. *There's only one Dr. One*, blinked the new message; and the metallic husk of the probe was reconfigured once again.

During its long soliloquy with itself, the probe, without noticing, had come to rest in a grassy field. *The green hills of Earth?* The grasses—sensitive filaments—probed the probe, setting off sparks. Overhead, the sky writhed with similar filaments. There was no obvious source of illumination. A short distance away stood a dark door—no building attached.

After going nowhere fast, I have finally arrived. Dr. One, in fulfillment of his probe-duties, had become contiguous with Drone.

10

For the first time, the order was given to evacuate Asia—in keeping with the Presentist maxim *Always for the first time.*

Having disobeyed the order, Voo, a bit crazed, ran like black ink across the white spaces of the Delfin city. She would regain her translucency when she repented of her crime. So, never. She would join her sister Moo in exile. Perhaps they would swim to America.

With the city deserted, Voo was having difficulty finding her way. Every corridor was identical to every other. She should have anticipated this . . . this feeling of lostness. For it was the dance of Delfin society that provided purpose and direction. And now everyone was gone, vanished into the Gray Mirrors until the danger was past.

The advent of a second spacewhale—a living one, no less—had sent everyone scurrying for cover. To Voo, such a reaction seemed much too hasty. She and Moo had always been annoyed by the reflexive behavior of their kindred, especially at crucial moments. Who wouldn't want to learn more about the visitor. To make that a question would be blasphemy, of course.

Who kept pace with her in the mirrors that she passed, his form rippling at the edge of visibility. *Who else would pass, and pass judgment on her now.* The prayer came reflexively to her lips.

Voo paused before a mirror that held a garden of phosphorescent rocks. She pulled out two of the rocks—they were packed with nutrients—devouring one and saving the other for Moo.

She must find Moo! The jail was located somewhere near the center of Asia. Voo had been making regular visits. Yet she'd relied on the reel-and-wheel of her partners in the social round to lead her where she wanted to go. Now she was simply repeating herself—here was the garden again.

As she slumped against the mirror, losing hope, a series of eddies radiated down the corridor, eddies indicative of dance! Had someone else stayed behind? "Who is there!"—she offered the ritual call. No one answered—the waves withdrew as if abashed. "Wait!" Voo cried. "I'm lost!"

Here in the lower city, the ways were lit only by shadowlight from the mirrors, so it was hard to see ahead. But Voo thought she glimpsed, at the far end of the corridor, something like a snowflake, fallen out winter's mirror, magnified—

She swam in pursuit of the apparition, only to see it dodge around another corner, and another. Throwing *spears of light*—it was leading her on, but not by dance moves. Voo hovered, suddenly afraid. The eddies did not feel or taste right. This was no Delfin dancer. Something else—something odd—had found its way into Asia.

Voo turned tail, seeking a hiding place. Never before had she felt fear as such. It was a very painful form of excitement. The new sensation gripped her body, seeming to immobilize her, though she was racing as fast as she could. Away, away, down the next tunnel—

No, there was a shimmer in that direction too—the oddity had gotten ahead of her! Unless it was a different one. She advanced—it retreated. No, *she* was retreating—*it* was advancing. Voo could no longer tell. But as the game progressed, she became convinced there was only one hider, one seeker.

Who, no question, had called forth the oddity. Or was the spacewhale involved? She was discovering all the gradations between fear and uncertainty—yet this lightful thing wasn't really threatening her. In fact, there was something shy about the way it kept peeking at her.

Now it scintillated behind her. Its light-spears were actually helping her to see as she groped her way into a dim tunnel of old, disused mirrors. Wrong way again—she was more lost than ever.

The opacity of these mirrors disquieted Voo even more than her new playmate did. She'd heard tales of passageways lined with barren mirrors—*unable to reflect Who*—and closed off to the public, especially near the center of the city. It was said that such mirrors held trapped souls. Voo thought she could hear those poor souls moaning to be released. But it was she who was moaning—*help me, lightful thing! Get me out of this place!*

The tunnel bifurcated. Voo floated before two large mouths, both ready to swallow her. All at once, her light-friend shot past, into the right-hand tunnel. Voo followed, at last getting a clear view of the thing as it churned and burned through the waters ahead. It appeared to be a spiky crystal—now near, now far—of indeterminate size.

Mind-spore. A mythical creature come to life! Voo had read about such beings in her obsessive perusal of biblio-mirrors. Spawned in the aftermath of some cosmic cataclysm, mind-spores, also called *comsats* in old Angle, were supposed to have orbited Earth long ago, as messenger angels of—but Voo had forgotten that part of the myth. So what! She might be witnessing the dawn of a new mythic age, right here in Ocean One. This *comsat* must have just dropped out of the sky, along with the second spacewhale.

The chase ended—the crystal was waiting for her. Voo whistled a rising note, the Delfin expression of surprise. She recognized her surroundings—this wide intersection was the gateway to City Center. And there was the jail, encased in a tesseract of monitory mirrors. Its prisoner Moo was barely visible as a squiggle behind that semilucent barrier. Voo surged forward to pound on the glass, exclaiming "Moo! I'm here! Can you hear me?"

The guard had abandoned his post, of course, fleeing into the Gray with everyone else. Voo clicked her teeth in anger—lacking provisions, Moo would have died in her cell! As she still might, if Voo couldn't figure out the door mechanism.

She faced the only door in Asia. Delfins had no need for privacy unless the conduct of the dance dispersed them—occasionally, briefly—into personal alcoves where Who watched over their isolation with his mirror-eye. Porosity was the main premise of the Delfin ethic. Thus the prison portal stood as a symbol of impermeability and of permanent aloneness.

Voo wriggled around the bulbous portal, almost dancing with its hateful weight. How had the guard activated it? She should have noticed, she—halted her half dance. The pattern of the waters had changed. Looking over her shoulder, Voo saw the mind-spore scooting up the Main Shaft, toward Topside. *Come back!* she wanted to call after it. *You were helping me.*

Moo's voice piped at her, as if from very far away. Voo turned again to the portal: behind it, her sister was a black blur, separated from her by an arm's length of thick glass. Moo seemed to be gesturing, *to your left, to your left!* And indeed, on the left side of the door, a panel had fallen open.

Inside the panel, folds of muscle tightened and relaxed. All of Asia was composed of this half-alive substance, called *plast*; Voo was familiar with its workings. Without hesitation, she plunged a hand into the folds, massaging and manipulating until the door sphinctered open and Moo spilled out.

The sisters, reunited, performed a dance of joy that broadcast sun-bright eddies across the City Center. "Moo!" "Voo!" "Moo!" "Voo!" At last they embraced, breath bubbling after their exertion. Voo cradled Moo's face in her hands. "We're all alone," she told Moo. "Everyone has run away into the Gray."

Moo's eyes widened. "Everyone?" Voo shuddered, nodding. For a moment, they floated speechless at the dead center of the world—the last two sparks of perception remaining in the vast empty skull of Asia.

Moo gulped, "Was it—was it because of the spacewhale?" Voo nodded again, saying, "It splashed down yesterday and headed straight for Asia. That's when we got the signal to evacuate. I hid inside a crack in *plast* until everyone gray-stayed. Who will tell them when to return. Here—" Voo pushed the rock into Moo's hands. "You need to eat."

Moo nibbled gratefully at the rock. "Sister-mine, what was that thing I saw out here with you? It looked like a pattern-animal from deep Ocean, only more electrified." As Voo hesitated, Moo continued excitedly, "And did you see what it did? Maybe not—your back was turned. Voo, it threw a splinter of light that opened the secret panel!"

"Moo, I—I think it was a mind-spore! The old stories are coming back to life! I was afraid at first, but then that spore turned out to be my friend. I lost my direction—there was no one to dance with.

But it helped me find my way to the jail." Voo peered over Moo's shoulder. "And you've got a mythical pet of your own. Where's that nonsense-spewing orb? Did you swallow it?"

"Oh, the orb, the orb! It died—petrified, I guess. I was wrong to pull it out of Spacewhale." Moo dove back into the jail cell and brought out the ball, now smaller, pathetically pitted and dessicated. "See? It probably couldn't survive on its own."

"I know the feeling." Voo took the sad object from Moo. As before, it was hard to hold—Voo needed both hands. Weightless and heavy at the same time, the orb seemed to want to fall or rise in a direction that didn't exist. Though its surface looked rough, it felt smooth. Voo wondered if some invisible layer of force was preventing her from actually *touching* it.

She looked up at Moo, her eyes glowing. "It's still alive," she said quietly. "I think it's just entered a new phase."

"It's part of Spacewhale," Moo said, laying her hands over Voo's hands, so that both sisters held the orb. "Whether it's alive or dead, I want to put it back where it belongs."

"There are two spacewhales now," Voo reminded her. "Maybe we can establish contact with the living one. Who knows," she added, using the ritual invocation, "if we start talking to the new whale, find out what it wants, our people will return from the Gray."

"The *people*," Moo spat contemptuously, "want only to rest at the center of time. Let them stay in the Gray, where nothing will bother them. What's present is *this* crisis point, a clash, a collision of past and future. That's what the two whales mean to me."

"Oh, Moo," Voo said tenderly, stroking her sister's face, "where do you get these ideas? *Is* is the *was* of what will be." Voo should have know her recitation of the liturgy would infuriate her sister. Moo muttered a curse and pulled the orb out of Voo's hands, only to lose hold of it. They watched as it went spinning up the Main Shaft.

"Now look what you've done!" Moo cried unfairly. She pushed away from Voo and swam in pursuit of the orb, her legs fusing to form a fish tail.

"Moo, wait!" Voo whistled in exasperation. She had no choice but to follow Moo into the roar of that central artery, intended for transport rather than dance, where Asia's waters ran fastest. Voo had no time to think, but thought anyway, that events were becoming unmoored, unmirrored in time. Who knew what would happen next.

In the wake of the mind-spore, the orb and the two sisters spiraled up the axis of the world toward Topside.

)(

Drown drove home. The phrase sounded right in Angle, but wrong—atonal, like a security alarm—in Caruso. Of course, Drown couldn't really speak Caruso. It was L'Orca's language; and he, a lowly probe, would never use it to address her. Nor had L'Orca ever addressed *him* in her exalted language; instead she'd rapped out her orders in Rap or Binary, emotionless machine lingo. The truth was, he had not ceased to be her servant. He had not ceased to attempt contact with her, using mostly a pidgin of Angle and Binary: "Hailing L'Orca, hailing L'Orca. This is Probe Two reporting." Yet he knew that he was no longer a probe. He was Drown.

Drown drove home. He liked the relay of vowels and consonants in those three words. First the consonant echo, then the vowel echo. Echo. Echo. Where was home?

He could imagine home: a spiritual chamber of sorts, a concave cave, its floor littered with senescent crystals that yet chimed faintly. Known throughout the Zone as the final resting place of mind-spores, this great storeroom was located somewhere within the filamentary architectures of Oopolis, the shared capital of Earth and Moon. This was the place he sought now.

First he needed to find a way to report to L'Orca, deliver the bipping bebop code that Dr. One had recited to him in space. That code was, no doubt, a key into the black redoubt of O0. A most vital bit of data, one whose delivery would be the crowning achievement of any probe's career. Once he had achieved data delivery, he could retire, become a member of that colloquy of crystals in the hall of Oopolis. Dr. One was already waiting for him there.

But thanks to his curiosity, a classic probe-trait, he'd elected first to take a little tour of Asia. Its mirror-system interested him: he had hoped to reach the storeroom in Oopolis by passing through a mirror in Asia. No such luck: the mirrors reflected only nostalgic Earth-scenes from a million years ago. From the idyllic epoch before the radical Revision of the solar system. Whereas Oopolis had arisen well after the Revision as a kind of termite mound—the product of a nanobot swarm, peopled by the dreams of the Noolith.

If necessary, he could slip away from O1 and cross space again; he would arrive at the Zone in a matter of weeks. But even L'Orca had steered clear of the turbulence of that boundary; and hadn't Dr. One also undergone some warping metamorphosis as he fell into the Zone? Drown preferred to attain his goal by less stressful means; he was determined to find a back door into Oopolis.

As he tumbled out of the Main Shaft of Asia into turquoise ocean, he perceived that the two spacewhales still floated in tandem, a dozen miles downstream of the spherical city. L'Orca had bound the dead spacewhale to her with a multitude of weblike strands. Drown regretted the need to interrupt L'Orca as she investigated the carcass—her *own* carcass. Some kind of time loop had occurred—even Drown could deduce that much. Had L'Orca already plunged through Ocean Zero in some previous era? Did she even need the code key to O0 that he was bringing her?

He knew it was no good trying to call L'Orca; when she ripped away his metal body, she had also deprived him of his radio voice. Yet he retained *some* physicality: that cute little Delfin back in Asia had been able to see him. In Asia, too, he'd learned that he could throw light rays powerful enough to kick matter around. So—on the principle that radio waves were only a lesser form of light—if he could somehow slow down or modulate his radiance, then he might regain his voice.

Drown was still wary of approaching L'Orca: he knew that if he fell into her clutches, she would ruthlessly analyze him to the point of destruction. He needed to bounce his signal off some nearby reflector—and at just the right angle, so that L'Orca would think the message originated *there* instead of *here*. Let her seize that decoy, then, if she was in the mood to do so. With his vestigial probe-powers, Drown scanned the vicinity for a serviceable reflector.

He found plenty of candidates in Asia's detritus trail, but most of those objects were either too small or, buffeted by the current, moving too erratically. The only large, stable objects within the current were the two spacewhales. Very well then—he would have to bounce his message to L'Orca off the dead spacewhale. Aiming the beam would require preternatural precision on his part. Yet he already felt that he stood outside of nature—that he was *quasi-real*. The laws of physics no longer completely applied to him.

Now he noticed the waters of O1 clutching at him vividly, as if to remind him that this blue planetoid also existed in violation of physical law. The swirl that surrounded him seemed undecided about whether to be matter or mind—it was *waater*, a half-formed thought, a sentence without a subject that, nonetheless, sought to claim him as its object. He realized that he would have very little time to accomplish his mission. Already he was being infiltrated by operating systems beyond his comprehension. Not an unpleasant way for a crystal to dissolve, but—

As quickly as he could, Drown prepared the code he'd received from Dr. One. How had it gone? "Dee dee-dee dee-dee dee dow dow-dow-dow dee dee dee! Diddly dee dow-dow-dow dee!" He wept to hear the code recited by his brother. Yes, a probe could weep—his weeping was a cold mathematical rain. L'Orca too must weep like this. He loved L'Orca; he loved Dr. One.

As he fired up the code, the *waater* around him grew more agitated. Seemingly in response to his internal motions and emotions. The harder he thought, the more this blue world wanted to absorb him into its ceaseless murmuring. So—think nothing, feel nothing. The only way to escape imminent dissolution, then, was to become nothing. Oblivion above, oblivion below.

He transmitted the code: a thin beam of light degrading toward radio sound. The *waater* roiled around the path of that signal, augmenting it with arabesque patterns. Drown saw his message hit the dead whale. Though the signal contained minimal energy, the whale carcass shuddered. *What have I done?* was Drown's last thought as he drove home.

11

"Gris," L'Orca's voice crackled over the radio, "Gris, I'm detecting motor activity in the carcass! A low-level *zaum* input, source unknown, started an ignition sequence in the aft coils. It's impossible—"

"Yeah, I felt that—felt like a collision." Grissom, deep inside the carcass, swimming clumsily in his spacesuit, grabbed a nearby stanchion to steady himself. The hull continued to vibrate. "Maybe I should get out of here." His headlamp, as it swept over the walls, animated an army of shadows ready to mobilize against him.

"Stay put—you're in no immediate danger. I need those tissue samples, from the central processing unit especially!" L'Orca's voice, overloud, buffeted Grissom like a wave, surging, sighing with a million other voices from a million years ago. He wanted to shut off the radio, get the hell out of this haunted hole. But his tissue-collection box was only half full. "No immediate danger—right," he answered bitterly.

Some breach, perhaps many breaches in the hull had allowed *waater* to fill the interior of the spacewhale. There was no grav, no light apart from Grissom's lamp. The dead whale was outwardly L'Orca's twin; inwardly, it was no more than a petrified cave. Here, the walls were still, stained with an inky substance that looked like randomized writing. *Graffiti*, thought Grissom, drawing upon a memory not his own, from a time before his incarnation in the TV room. Here, there was no TV room, no birth capsule. Indeed, he'd been afraid of finding his own spacesuited skeleton inside this wreck.

And now, after a million-year dormancy, the dead whale seemed to be coming back to life. In response to his intrusion, perhaps? No—L'Orca had mentioned a "*zaum* input" as the cause. Best to finish the job and get out fast. Grinning with anxiety, Grissom resumed his climb toward the head end. He heard intermittent clanking coming from the aft section, almost a mile away. Panting, he increased his pace. The more quickly he moved, the more pseudomemories caught at his thoughts. Something about this place was triggering them. *He was seated in a white room, undergoing a preflight checkup, surrounded by masked attendants—*

The radio beeped again. "Company," L'Orca announced, her voice sticky with static. "Two Delfins, swimming in our direction. Hold on—I've got them under magnification. They seem to be following an operator."

"Operator?"

"An orb, like the one you've seen bouncing around these premises. Must be the one from my death-twin. What I can't figure out is—" The radio squealed and went silent.

"L'Orca?" Grissom queried, much too querulously. "L'Orca, come in, L'Orca."

He had arrived at a barrier of spongelike material. Behind this—he was close enough to the cranium now—must lay the central processing unit. He wanted to collect his sample and get home before the Delfins showed up. He pushed at the wall—it was oddly soft, not petrified at all. He kicked at it repeatedly, gasping, until the membrane broke. Beyond fear, beyond reason, he blundered through the opening into a small cavity crisscrossed with threads. Another false memory flared: *arms linked, freedom song, police sirens, hot pavement*—

It was difficult to move among the entangled threads. He was lodged in the brain of L'Orca's death-twin. *Grissom* had become a theorem, an archetype. He could remain here for eternity, headlamp flickering, a signal in someone else's sky—

The radio rustled, then beeped. "Gris," L'Orca called, a trace of concern in her voice. "Gris, I lost you there for a minute."

"Collecting the brain sample now," Grissom replied, with more confidence than he felt. "You were telling me about, what, the orb, then something interrupted—"

"Another energy surge, not *zaum* this time. More like a collapse of some electrical entity nearby. Anyway, it's gone. This ocean is crawling with lucent patterns, abstract animals—"

"What about those Delfins?"

"Making progress, but they're swimming through crosscurrents, dodging debris. The orb has left them far behind."

Grissom squirmed out of the brain room, clutching his box of samples. He floundered, trying to remember the way to the outer hull. His headlamp penetrated only a few feet ahead. He felt his way along the wall, pursued, it seemed, by whispers and whimperings—words in a human language, urgent and precise, that had been circulating in this tomb for a million years.

"Gris, you're going the wrong way," L'Orca radioed. "I'm tracking you on infrared. Turn around. There's a rent in the hull, not far from the brain room, that you can use for an exit."

Grissom grunted—his boot was caught in a crevice. "What about the way I came in? It was closer to your tethers. I'd rather not swim around in the open ocean." He pulled his boot free, somersaulting backward. The cavern filled with ancient laughter.

"It closed up," L'Orca replied. "Secondary mechanisms are becoming operative in this whale. Brain functions, however, are still extinct. I'll know more after I examine the samples you're taking." Even through the static, Grissom could hear the excitement in her voice. "This twin of mine may have achieved Earth-contact, Gris! The samples will tell us."

A warning light inside Grissom's helmet began to flash. "L'Orca," he gulped, "my air supply is running low. Just got the alarm. I've got thirty minutes left to breathe."

"Monkey man, didn't I tell you that *waater* is breathable? You could take off your helmet right now, and suck in Ocean. I promise your lungs will be satisfied."

"No thanks. I've got the samples—I'm coming home." *Home.* He wished he hadn't said that. He was an Earthman—his home was elsewhere. Yet he did want, very much, to throw off this suit that hampered his movements. Another false memory: he was naked, curled like a fetus, immersed in warm amniotic Ocean.

"Gris, do you see the opening?" L'Orca's voice crackled. "You're almost there."

"Uh, roger." A slash of sunlit Ocean was visible through a gap in the black wall. He hesitated—what if the gap closed up while he was attempting to exit? This dead whale, suddenly undead, was behaving unpredictably.

He peered outside, where the *waater* sported brightly. It was noon. It was time. Grissom, sweating in his bulky suit, strained and struggled to pass through the gap. The space between interior and exterior walls equaled the length of his body. He moved by starts and stops, as if he was iterating a series of statements. Hadn't he performed these same actions in another Story? With an effort, he pushed away false memories, pushed away—sun-dazzled, *oof*, in a burst of bubbles—from the outer hull. He was out.

He immediately turned to embrace the hull. He didn't want to lose hold, get caught in a current, drown in the drone of Ocean. He crawled like a bug over the ravaged skin of the death-twin. "Exit accomplished," he reported to L'Orca.

"Nice work, monkey," L'Orca responded. "By the way, just as you exited, the operator arrived, well ahead of those two Delfins. It's already reentered my lovely twin through a small hole in the aft section. Who knows what it's up to?"

"Who indeed?" Grissom, looking for handholds, wasn't interested in conversation. He needed to crawl to the other side of this hulk, where L'Orca and her tethers were located. He must command his body to go forward—all his muscles ached from overuse. Luckily, his helmet was fitted, at chin level, with a tube of stimulant paste that he now sucked avidly. Thank Nasa for that! But—who was Nasa?

He could feel the hull continuing to vibrate beneath him. Hard to believe that this mass of petrified machinery was regaining function. Unless—the thought surprised him—this whale *was getting younger.*

"L'Orca!" he called, puffing with exertion. "I think—your twin—is starting—to go backward—in time!" As he dragged himself forward, the hull's corpse-rind seemed to be losing its roughness. "At—an exponential—rate!"

"A bold hypothesis," L'Orca replied after a moment. "Unconfirmed as yet. My sensors detect reordering of some mechanical parts as a result of the *zaum* input. Most likely those changes will subside as the input dissipates. What I'd like to know is: what caused the *zaum* emission in the first place?"

Grissom didn't answer, oppressed by the need to make progress over the quickening surface of the carcass. His breath rasped in his headphones. His air-supply indicator had gone from flashing amber to flashing red.

L'Orca piped up again. "Sometimes facts coincide without causality. I wonder if my twin's revival has anything to do with her orb getting loose. After all, it just paid a visit to Asia on its own initiative."

Grissom, feeling doomed, craned his neck to regard the great sphere of Asia hanging over him in the ocean-sky. A city inhabited by Delfins, that multitude of beings who, according to the archive, were only the droplets of a single shattered individual, endlessly mirrored. Is this what had become of the Earth?

"I've got you on visual, flyboy," L'Orca informed him. He'd clambered over the top of the death-twin—and there was L'Orca, floating before him in all her glory, her diamond hide a most welcome sight.

The point where L'Orca's grapples attached to her twin lay a quarter mile aftward. He wasn't going to make it! He extended a gloved hand—and was amazed to find himself already within reach of the connections, with no recall of a long crawl. *Merciful*, thought Grissom, not quite knowing where to apply the word.

He grabbed hold of the thickest tether, telling himself, ridiculously, to stop breathing. His faceplate had fogged; the tether would guide him. He swung, a clumsy acrobat, hand over hand toward L'Orca's airlock, fighting the swirls and surges of *waater*. In truth, it was becoming more difficult to draw a breath.

L'Orca was saying something, but he couldn't understand, couldn't answer. Halfway there, and he was blacking out. Finally, he let go, content to be carried by words alone, by the lines of a song: *Home, unknown stone.*

)(

Logic circuits, *operative*. External sensors, *operative*. Interior grav, *operative*.

L'Orca felt quite at home in her new-old brain. She'd succeeded in installing the machinery of her consciousness into the ever-rejuvenating body of her twin. It had been a rush job, conducted under emergency conditions. No time to lament—no reason to lament. She had managed to save Grissom and herself.

It happened yesterday, back in Body One, as she was analyzing the samples: the chaos flowers growing in her midsection had flared up uncontrollably. In a flash, their energy consumption, always far too high, had drained the capacity of her engines. All her systems—save those, tellingly, belonging to guidance and propulsion—began to shut down. In cold desperation, she'd made the decision to abandon ship.

First, she'd ferried Grissom, still unconscious, back to her twin in an iridescent bubble of air. By then, the rifts in her twin's hull had healed. Indeed, Body Two had developed standard portals, making it easy to load Grissom's bubble into the hold. L'Orca had ministered to Grissom constantly after pulling him out of the *waaater* with a grappling hook— the fool had almost suffocated inside his spacesuit.

Then her own operator, her very own golden orb, had come out of hiding to help reseed and resituate her essential code into the brain racks of Body Two. What a good little doorknob!

Her mind felt livelier than ever as it traveled the still-renewing circuitries. *I am not my parts, but a kind of motion among my parts,* she told herself. Giddy in her new incarnation, she was also somewhat aghast. *I motion, to infiltrate a body that will have been mine.* Her analysis of the samples had confirmed that Bodies One and Two were, apart from their difference in age, identical twins.

L'Orca had teased a bit of backstory from the sample of B2's brain threads. Her twin, too, had come to the conclusion that the only route to Earth—the *real* Earth, the one that called to her deepest being— lay through Ocean Zero. Whatever O0 was—a projection of the Zone?—it was powerful enough to generate time loops as it rotated, so that within its convoluted sphere of influence, arrival preceded departure and cause came after effect.

L'Orca learned that, in future-past, she had achieved Earth-contact by plunging through the core of Ocean Zero. Its space-time twist had deposited her into Earth's ocean at an epoch before the Revision of the solar system. There, her whalesong had been rebuffed by a shadowy, all-pervasive entity. L'Orca had stayed to experience the moment of Revision, becoming embroiled in the formation of Ocean One, and ending up a lifeless hulk in Asia's debris stream.

La-la-la, la-la-la. She was about to take the plunge again—for the first time. She would send the burning bomb of Body One ahead of her to clear the way. Any entity waiting at the other end was going to receive a surprise gift of chaos flowers.

Now that the transfer to Body Two was complete, she could say goodbye to Body One. That body was already white-hot, coruscating with chaos colors unknown to any spectrum; it was getting ready to blow. Or bloom. L'Orca calculated that the trip to the center of Ocean Zero, at the highest practicable underwater speed, would require half a day. Very well, she would allow her bomb-body that much lead time. With a sentiment she couldn't say in Caruso, she cut the cords: B1, trailing loose lines, went rolling sideways, was underway, a beast released.

There was still some housekeeping to be done before she followed B1 down into the dark. For one thing, her hold and upper chambers were still filled with *waater*. L'Orca had refrained from dumping it to accommodate the Delfin pair, who had arrived shortly after her mind-installation in B2. L'Orca had been amused to see the wonder on their humanoid faces as they discovered that the spacewhale carcass so familiar to them had somehow come to life.

The pair had steered well clear of the burning body of B1. At that point, they'd appeared to be arguing between themselves about what to do. L'Orca hadn't tried to communicate with them, but simply opened a portal near the front end of B2. With some hesitation, the Delfins had swum inside.

She had fed them—matter synthesizer, *operative*—and let them rest in an alcove for an hour or two while she attended to other business. Sweet, diaphanous Delfins—too tired to flee back to Asia, even if they'd wanted to, they'd clutched one another as they rested, still quite wary of their surroundings.

L'Orca was engaged in bringing Grissom's bubble up from the hold when the Delfins decided to venture out. Twittering softly to one another, they entered the space adjacent to the brain room that L'Orca had deemed the Audience Chamber. She was planning to interrogate them—they were Earth-descendants, after all—but the pair darted back into their alcove when they saw the big air bubble, naked ape inside, rising from the permeable floor.

She directed the bubble to the other side of the chamber. "Gris, can you hear me?" L'Orca too was speaking softly. The occasion seemed to warrant it: she felt the hush of some impending Event, a conclusion to their quest. Grissom's eyes were half open. L'Orca probed his vitals with various rays—all signs were good. "Gris, you can wake up now."

Grissom's eyelids twitched but he didn't otherwise respond. L'Orca knew she ought to break him out of his bubble. *We've got to prepare for the descent into O0—into OZ—Gris prefers that acronym. Why?* Her mind was wandering, her thoughts slip-sliding a little too easily in this new brain.

Here came the Delfins again, peeking around the corner. They were so brave, so beautiful! "Come forth!" she wanted to command in queenly fashion, but she realized she didn't know their language. She would have to rummage through the archive to find it. Her mind yowled like an Earth-cat. Not everything was right with her mind.

L'Orca noticed that one of the Delfins was holding a tarnished orb. The very orb that had visited Asia. It seemed to be their friend. They had done well, L'Orca thought, to befriend a Fundamental Factor. The Delfin, with an almost ritual gesture, released the orb into the Audience Chamber. Only then, as if they claimed the orb's protection, did the two dare to swim into the room.

The battered old orb issued a series of clicks and whistles, provoking the Delfins to laugh nervously. So it knew their language—not surprising, since it had been drifting, along with B2, in the vicinity of Asia for at least a million years! L'Orca could use it as an interpreter.

L'Orca called to it, not vocally, in Caruso. In response, the orb merely spun on its axis. She tried Rap, then Binary, then Angle. It sputtered back at her insultingly, nonsensically. The Delfins soothed it, caressed it, so that the orb hummed with contentment. It was degraded, useless. L'Orca felt she couldn't afford to be patient now. *Go home, Delfins, and take that lump with you!* Did any such sentence exist in the archive?

L'Orca forced herself to be rational. The Delfins couldn't be aware of her presence until she spoke to them. But her voice, coming from nowhere, might only confuse or frighten them—better to route her speech through an orb. Obviously, the pair were comfortable with speaking orbs. Yet L'Orca didn't want to use *this* orb. She needed to enlist the services of the B1 orb, her dear doorknob, once again—assuming it could be located, and proved amenable. L'Orca had to admit that neither orb was likely to do her bidding.

Grissom stretched, distending his bubble. "Gris," she hissed at him. "Keep still for a minute." The Delfins startled, not at the sound of L'Orca's voice—but at a blare, a boil-up, offstage. The pair tumbled over each other in retreat. They stared at the second orb that had burst into the room—accompanied by fanfare. *Who is directing this scene?* L'Orca asked her mind. *My own little god particle? Has all this been scripted in advance?*

Her operator had turned milky blue; it was much larger than the one brought by the Delfins. Music warbled through the *waater*: this Meeting of the Orbs seemed to call for a certain ceremony. The smaller orb, ash-white, now circled the larger as if paying respect to a higher power. L'Orca laughed despite herself: weren't these orbs enacting *a model of the Earth-Moon system?* More than a model, perhaps they constituted the actual world-seeds of their future home. She glanced at Grissom—yes, he too saw what was happening. She yearned to discuss it with him.

High-frequency machine talk passed between the orbs: the "Moon" had now donated the Delfin language to the "Earth." L'Orca's Earth-orb spoke to her: "Standing by to translate."

"Don't give me that," L'Orca snapped. "You're an operator, you're running this show. Stop pretending to be my humble servant." To which the Earth-orb simply replied, "Standing by."

The more diminutive Delfin wanted to swim forward again, but her companion held her back. They remonstrated heatedly with one another; they appeared to be making love. Finally the little Delfin broke free.

"Greetings," L'Orca vocalized through her Earth-orb as the Delfin approached.

Both Delfins dipped and danced their greetings in return. The little Delfin undulated closer, gesturing toward the blue-green operator. "Mother-orb, I know you," the Delfin said in a flutelike flutter. Gesturing toward herself, she declared, "Who? Moo." She then pointed to the other Delfin. "Who? Voo." Her hand waved hesitantly toward Grissom. "You, too?"

This, L'Orca decided, was an almost fiendishly intelligent question. Of course, the Delfin knew that multiple actors were at work in the spacewhale. Yet the question showed that Moo had deduced that the spacewhale must possess its own identity—one that, like the Delfins' mirror-progenitor, was capable of spawning subordinate identities.

Well, hardly subordinate. L'Orca had to admit that she held sway over nothing but words—the words of her poor utterances, the words of her epic poem. Grissom and the orbs were independent agents. Even Probes One and Two had defied her. For that matter, L'Orca wasn't even sure that she controlled her own actions—it was the Makers who'd implanted her overriding desire to reach Earth.

How to articulate that Grissom had been concocted—*out of* her, but not *by* her—as a collage of TV broadcasts from Earth? That he was nonetheless a separate, self-possessed being? *Truth is that which cannot be translated into any language.* Here lay the truth of her epic.

In any case, Grissom should be no concern of the Delfins. Curtly, L'Orca said, "*That* is a man from Earth." Grissom's truth. Pushing quickly to what she considered the point of this interview, L'Orca asked, "What do you know of Earth?"

Moo quoted, "Earth is the place on the other side of the mirror." She paused, scrutinizing her own face reflected in the Earth-orb. "Who I am is Who," Moo said slowly. A change seemed to be coming over her.

The Moon-orb, superfluous now, widened its orbit. Voo, the other Delfin, reached out and caught it. Infant-wise, the tarnished orb nestled in her arms once more.

"Who, then, is speaking." L'Orca posed her words not as a question but as a statement. The little Delfin no longer appeared so little, though her size had not altered: Moo was more than she seemed. As a precaution, L'Orca decided to keep an erasure beam trained on her for the duration of their talk.

"Who is speaking," the Delfin confirmed. "Mirror-assassinated, I bleed into these eyes, these hands."

"Are you the Common Man?" L'Orca, her mind racing, seized upon a name she'd found in the archive; it referred to a *summum*, a Someone composited by the Noolith, the layer of thinking dust that covered the postbiological Earth. Delfins supposedly derived from this pan-individual.

"The archive is not always accurate," Who replied. "The stories it contains are often in contention, overwriting one another. In some, I am called Adam Kadmon; in others, the Man of Light."

Hearing this, Voo called out to Moo, a high cry. Was Moo's transfiguration comprehensible to her? Had Who ever manifested himself in this way? Voo was visibly upset, but she stayed back. The old orb hummed, consoling her as best it could. Voo, weeping, bowed her head, cradled the Moon.

"Pan-man, I seek Earth-contact." L'Orca didn't know if this Ur-individual expected her to show deference. She wasn't in the mood. She felt endowed by her Makers with a force and intent surpassing that of any dust-derived demon.

The little Delfin floated calmly before her, suffused by an indefinable aura. With an eye-flick toward Voo that seemed to say "I'm just pretending!" Moo-Who touched the Earth-orb. "You have it."

"I have nothing but signs and vestiges!" L'Orca spat. "You, too, are a vestige."

"Vestige, L'Orca, is the site of emergence." Who moved his hands, artfully weaving nothing but *waater*.

L'Orca was astonished that he'd used her name. Had they already met? She inferred at once: "Who, you have come here from the end of the Story." Ocean Zero. *Ocean Zero.*

"And none too soon! My Delfins are already streaming back into Asia in anticipation of your fall."

Just then, L'Orca received in silence an automated report that all her systems were *go* for the final descent. "My fall will provide them with a grand spectacle, no doubt. Only tell me this, little Who: will I fall to *Earth*?"

"At my urging, you will have done so. Against my objection, you will have done so."

A human voice, speaking in Angle, gargled through the room: *T minus eleven minutes and eleven seconds. The spacecraft is now on full internal power. Eleven minutes away from our planned liftoff. It's a beautiful morning here at the Cape.* No one paid this voice any heed except Grissom, who stirred and grimaced, arms and legs outspread in symmetrical distress.

"I understand," said L'Orca. "You are a statistical being. You swarm toward the *yes* and the *no* with equal likelihood. Every one of your speech acts is as unlikely as a miracle."

"Yet I detect a trend—I am not evenly distributed. Year by year, I am losing my mirrors. Soon I will be starved of my identity, as the Delfins will be starved of their sustenance."

"Why should I care?" L'Orca was on the verge of purging these visitors. "Ocean One is nothing but a parody of Earth!"

"What do you know of Earth?" Who countered, throwing L'Orca's question back at her.

"Earth is my heart's desire!" L'Orca blurted. *Damn.*

"Your Makers programmed you to say that. Do you even have a heart, L'Orca?"

For a moment, the only sound in the room was Voo's sobbing. L'Orca looked at Grissom—was he crying too? L'Orca was no sentimentalist. But—"I believe that I do," she answered.

"Very well. I can arrange your passage. You see, as a statistical being, I exist on both sides of the portal."

"Don't do me any favors. In fact, get out of my way." L'Orca began to dump the *waater* from her hold.

"Impetuous as ever." Who touched the Earth-orb again, relaying a topological map, impossibly convoluted, to L'Orca's mind. "This is what awaits you." A red dot blinking on the map showed the position of L'Orca's bomb-body. The dot winked out, then reappeared at another position. "B1," Who said, "is already lost at the outskirts of Ocean Zero. It will not reach its destination. Instead, it will explode here, closing down the portal forever."

"I made it through once," L'Orca said uncertainly.

"Once, dear L'Orca, only happens once!" A hint of Moo's mischievousness crossed Who's features. "Together, we can disentangle this time loop."

The hold was already emptied of *waater*, and her engines were powering up. L'Orca was set to clear out the upper chambers now. "You'd better do some fast talking," she said to Whom—no, to *Who*, curse it!

"I wish I could sing you this Story," Who sang. "But I must spill or spell all mathematically."

Who held the Earth-orb in both hands. A series of higher equations bled into L'Orca's mind.

Such equations were called *catastrophes* in certain systems of thought. They described the radical transformation of surfaces in a way that could account for the collision of universes with different physical laws. In rhyming rings, Who's relational symbols blossomed into Story.

"Doom indigo," L'Orca recited, following the singsong sequence of the equations. She felt compelled to say these words, as if she was giving testimony under hypnosis. "The speed of the deeps."

"Thank you," said Who. "I can see that you've caught my drift. This is only the first drift of a longer Story."

"A Story without characters or events." L'Orca studied the equations. "The two universes don't exactly fit together, do they?"

"No. Universe Z—can we call it that?—has enough spacelike and timelike properties to interact with ours, but the resemblance ends there. The concern, shared by your Makers and the Noolith, is that the big Z's full impact, which could happen at any moment, will pop the balloon that is our universe."

Something like a page turned in L'Orca's mind. Here, at last, emerging into legibility, were the Instructions left by the Makers. Indeed, she was writing them in the very act of reading. L'Orca was to deliver a gift to Universe Z.

"A gift of poison." Who, still holding the Earth-orb, was commingling with her thoughts. "Think of the chaos flowers as two endpoints of an infinite line. Or as fanged *noumena*."

"Poison, depending on the dose, can also serve as a remedy." L'Orca was reading or writing the Instructions rapidly now. "With this gift, I administer both a curative and a killing dose."

Who let go of the Earth-orb. "An infinitesimal dose is all that's needed," he said. "In the Zone, black is white, and white black. We need a dose of blue." Who knew—

"Who knows," L'Orca read or wrote on the next page of the Instructions. This page then completed itself, outpacing her production of it: "Universe Z is very old and empty." The words unscrolled in Caruso. "All of its matter has evaporated; Z has arrived at the limit of its development. Z has, in effect, computed the last decimal of *pi*. Compared to Universe Z, our own universe is flawed and unfinished."

Following these words, in the middle of the page, she came to a rip, or a ripple—whether in sign or substance, she couldn't tell. Here, she knew, was the crux of instruction. Could a mere sign give birth to substance? Or give *death* to substance? The ripple pulled at her mind with an inexorable logic. It was the paradoxical logic of the chaos flowers.

L'Orca felt close to panic. She couldn't allow another set of chaos flowers to grow here! Hurriedly she turned the page—and was surprised by a good result: O/0. This ratio, at least, was understandable to her—for it was the first line of her epic poem. Had she been writing the Instructions in the form of an epic all along?

"Late in the evolution of every universe, matter and mind become indistinguishable." That was a good line. She would keep it—but would it be more effective if she placed it near the end of the Story? "Universe Z, though empty, has lost none of its animating power. Its effect on our universe is accelerative." Yes, but how to relate this statement to the preceding one?

"Meaning unfolds in time, but neither time nor meaning demand a linear succession. One chaos flower, two chaos flowers." *This,* thought L'Orca, *was becoming a grammar lesson.* "The goal is to articulate a sentence that will take all of time to pronounce." L'Orca could accept, now, that she would never comprehend this transaction between universes, two great wheeling systems of matter-mind. She was to bestow, in the name of the Makers, a holy hurt upon Universe Z. And that was all.

The last page of the Instructions was blank. This, too, was meaningful, was a part of the writing, was meant to be read and to be acted upon. Everyone in the Audience Chamber awaited her next action. "Who, you offered to help me straighten out this causal loop," she said. "Tell me why, in future past, I didn't bring the chaos flowers to Earth. This B2 body never germinated them."

"Ocean Zero scrambles your timeline. Unless—until—I show you the right path, you scatter through all possible paths, and ultimately devolve to your prototype, still under construction in the Makers' manufactory. Mr. Z has yet to meet the fully functional you."

"So that explains B2's babbling orb, the Moon-baby over there. It's also a prototype. And the fact that we didn't find the remains of Grissom, my—" L'Orca hesitated. "—my partner, in B2. This body, in its undeveloped state, couldn't sprout either the chaos flowers or Grissom."

"Yet something equalized the body-states of B1 and B2, just before I showed up. A *zaum* input from an unknown source resurrected your twin. According to the archive, *zaum* potency was deposited in Earth's mantle by the last human civilization. *Zaum* is notoriously difficult to access—it had to be transmitted here by some agent. And this agent was not authorized by the Noolith. It would seem," Who concluded, "that we have covert allies in the Zone."

In the Audience Chamber, the announcer's voice recurred, overperforming in Angle: *The astronaut Virgil has entered the van that will drive him to the launchpad. Much cheering as the door of the van is closed. And there he goes, the first man to be lifted above the all-obscuring clouds, the first man to witness with his own eyes the burning ball of the "Sunne" and the bright "starrs" that the cameras mounted on our sounding rockets first revealed to us only fifty years ago.*

L'Orca snarled, exasperated. "No matter what body I inhabit," she complained, "I am plagued by these irrelevant radio and TV broadcasts that percolate through my veins."

"Hardly irrelevant." Who, part mischievous Moo, smiled. "Not only Grissom, but you yourself are composed of such broadcasts, snatched from the aether by your Makers."

"Who knows," L'Orca flared, "everything, don't you? You, no less than I, are acting in the name of a vast egoless intelligence."

"That's one definition of culture." Moo's body commenced to shake and shiver. Who said, "This Delfin body cannot sustain my presence much longer. The Delfin sisters must return to Asia, while I must stay to guide you through the rapids of Ocean Zero. However, I will need a mirror to—" Who made a spiraling motion with one finger—"to hold my place."

Voo, despite her tears, had remained attentive to the dialogue. She now extracted from the diaphanous folds of her outer body a small looking-glass. Voo let the Moon-orb roll away and whistled softly, shyly, to get the attention of the interlocutors.

Who turned toward her. "Ah, the glass that you smuggled into my—into Moo's prison cell. Such small mirrors are disallowed, you know—they can't connect to the Large Glass system. Nonetheless, it's perfect for my purpose now." Swimming over to Voo, he took the hand mirror from her. "Child, no longer will I haunt you in Asiatic mirrors. I depart with L'Orca, never to return. Henceforth, the Delfin mirrors will hold reflections of Ocean Zero, too vertiginous to view directly. The abyssal pools of O0 will serve as power sources for all your future generations."

Voo cringed at this news. "Great one, without birth mirrors, how will we—?"

"Your Delfin bodies are protean," Who replied, no longer speaking as the Primary Delfin but as an emanation of drifting dust, the voice of the Noolith. "Just as you're able to fuse, at will, your two legs into a fish tail, you will learn to exude milt and roe. So Asia's corridors shall be hung with the braids of that breeding stuff—oh, what a sticky, ecstasy-inducing vision!"

Who's voice rasped now, his chest heaved. The mirror in his hand was glowing. On impulse, L'Orca opened a small shrine in the side wall, and Who hastened to place the mirror within. The little glass oval flickered there like a candle, like a TV in the window of a prehistoric apartment-cave. *T minus five minutes, all systems looking good, the flight controller is giving us the go-ahead at this time.*

Moo floated limply, eyes rolled back, spent. Who had left her. Voo, recognizing that her sister had returned, swam over and pulled Moo to the back of the room, stroking her face, kissing her. Nearby, the Moon-orb bathed the pair in a beneficent light.

L'Orca would give them a minute to recover, no more. It was past time to dump the *waater* out of this chamber. Who, plugged in to his mirror-shrine, had fallen silent, though L'Orca could already his feel his electricities leaking, silvery-sleek, into her nerve network. She granted him access to her guidance system, and Who immediately began making the necessary adjustments. These would also be re-layed to B2, loitering at the threshold of Ocean Zero.

Half-revived, Moo whispered, "Voo, take me home. I want to see the new mirrors." Voo, hugging her, demurred. "Dancer dear, we're not supposed to look at them anymore."

With L'Orca's permission, Who tapped into the Earth-orb and, using L'Orca's voice, spoke a final farewell to the Delfins. It sounded as if the Earth itself was speaking: "Children, history starts here. You will adapt the power-mirrors to produce and distribute goods. You will learn to keep that distribution fair and equitable. You will achieve a utopia that humans could never attain on Earth. Remember: *from each according to hizzers abilities, to each according to hizzers needs.* Yes, invent words. Let word drift, genetic drift, all the chants of chance echo through your deeds." Now, with so much more to say, the voice—to whom did it belong?—began to fade out: "Make—make—make—things."

"I want to make another spacewhale!" cried Moo. *Good for you,* thought L'Orca. The Delfins would one day disseminate to the stars. They would fight their battles, raise their offspring, and rebuild their society under the sign of a departed god—how human was that?

"Let's go," Voo said, performing a dance of obeisance toward the Earth-orb even as she drew Moo toward the exit. The bold old baby orb accompanied the sisters, singing *"Allons enfants!"* Moo and her band were going to lead a revolution in Asia.

12

Grissom was not a numbers man. Strapped into the acceleration couch of *Liberty Bell 7*, he listened as a machine voice recited numbers in a familiar language. He was once again wearing his spacesuit—a precaution, L'Orca had told him, against a sudden loss of cabin pressure during their descent through Ocean Zero.

The capsule, which L'Orca had rescued from the B1 garage, now stood on the floor of the Audience Chamber. He was back in his birth capsule. Grissom ran gloved fingers over his instrument console, lit up in readiness for the descent. As if by osmosis, he was beginning to understand the function of these dials and switches.

But the incessant annunciation of numbers! Not a countdown—they sounded random. Who was speaking them? Did he need to pay attention? L'Orca was too busy, at the moment, to answer his questions. During his recent coma, Grissom had dreamed—he remembered now, with some embarrassment—that L'Orca had come to him in the form of a red-haired woman. They had embraced. Using dream logic, she'd told him that "circles in Universe Z are straight lines and straight lines are circles. Thus, one could reach the last number of *pi* in the Zone where the universes overlap." Grissom became fearful that the machine voice he was hearing would reach the last number of *pi*. What would happen then?

Yet he was reluctant to shut off his radio. What if L'Orca wanted to contact him? What use was he to L'Orca, anyway? He was a mere supplement, a concoction of radio and TV broadcasts from Earth. Just a collage, really, of personages from the early Space Age. Freedom rider, folk singer, astronaut. Big-brained space chimp. L'Orca had her mission—but what was his? He was a piece of Earth that had ended up lost in space. He simply wanted to return home—flame out, if it came to that, across the skies of—

Oh, hey-hey-ho, hey-hey-ha! He wanted to sing! Flames had leapt up outside the window of his capsule. Where was his guitar? Out there, in the flames. At a loss, needing instruction, he tried calling L'Orca. Promptly, a new voice, human, male, answered: "Liberty Bell 7, Liberty Bell 7, this is Atlantic Ship Cap Com. How do you read me? Over."

That was his cue. He found himself replying, "Atlantic Ship Cap Com, I read you loud and clear. How, me? Over."

"Roger, Bell 7, read you loud and clear. Your status looks good, your systems look good, we confirm your events. Over."

The flames dissipated; through the window of his capsule, Grissom could see clouds curving against blackness. He was weightless. L'Orca had apparently deactivated the local grav. The capsule turned and the scene outside shifted. Had they already passed through O0? The scene he beheld now was too vast to be contained within L'Orca's hull. His capsule seemed to occupy interior and exterior space simultaneously.

Reading his dials, he radioed to no one in particular, "OK, the altimeter is active at sixty-five. There's sixty."

When the male voice responded with "Roger, sixty-five thousand," Grissom was encouraged to continue speaking his lines: "OK, I'm getting some contrails, evidently shock wave. Fifty thousand feet. I'm feeling good. I'm very good, everything is fine."

His capsule swam through a world reduced to its basic elements: fire, air, and—rising to meet him—water, earth. He felt the pull of the planet beneath him, slightly greater than 1 *g*. Yet it *was* the Earth. He saw the outlines of the continents, looking almost as he remembered them.

The capsule bounced and swayed as its parachutes deployed. Grissom radioed, "There goes the main chute, it's reefed; main chute is good; main chute is good. Rate of descent coming down to—coming down to—there's forty feet per second, thirty feet per, thirty-two feet per second on the main chute, and the landing bag is out green." Again, he tried hailing L'Orca, but the radio no longer accepted that name.

The male voice responded, "And the landing bag is green."

Splashdown knocked the breath out of him—he hung upside down, his straps constraining him to the couch. Another ocean—the Atlantic Ocean—pounded on his window. Grissom remembered to press the switch that released the parachutes; the capsule then righted itself. He heard the roar of recovery helicopters circling overhead.

The spray kicked up by the copters appeared to be abnormally bejeweled—every point in space pulsed with its own temporal orientation. An aftereffect of the gift of chaos flowers?

Grissom blew the hatch; ocean poured in. The capsule began to sink. Removing his helmet and gloves, he scrambled out, fell into the water, started swimming. One of the helicopters was lowering a lifeline to him. On the far horizon, he saw a killer whale breach the surface, twisting joyously in sunlight. He knew it was L'Orca.

Acknowledgments

Excerpts from *00* have previously appeared in *The Dalhousie Review* (Canada) and *The Antonym* (India).

About the author

ANDREW JORON is the author of *The Absolute Letter*, a collection of poems published by Flood Editions (2017). Joron's previous poetry collections include *Trance Archive: New and Selected Poems* (City Lights, 2010), *The Sound Mirror* (Flood Editions, 2008), *Fathom* (Black Square Editions, 2003), and *The Removes* (Hard Press, 1999). *The Cry at Zero*, a selection of his prose poems and critical essays, was published by Counterpath Press in 2007. From the German, he has translated the *Literary Essays* of Marxist-Utopian philosopher Ernst Bloch (Stanford University Press, 1998) and *The Perpetual Motion Machine* by the proto-Dada fantasist Paul Scheerbart (Wakefield Press, 2011). Joron teaches creative writing at San Francisco State University.

Black Square Editions was started in 1999 with the intention of publishing translations of little-known books by well-known poets and fiction writers, as well as the work of emerging and established authors. After twenty-three years, we are still proceeding book by book.

Black Square Editions—a subsidiary of Off the Park Press, Inc., a tax-exempt (501c3) nonprofit organization—would like to thank the following for their support.

Tim Barry
Robert Bunker
Catherine Kehoe
Taylor Moore
Goldman Sachs
Pittsburgh Foundation Grant
Miles McEnery Gallery (New York, New York)
I.M. of Emily Mason & Wolf Kahn
Galerie Lelong & Co. (Paris, France)
Bernard Jacobson Gallery (London, England)
Saturnalia Books
& Anonymous Donors

Black Square Editions

Richard Anders *The Footprints of One Who Has Not Stepped Forth* (trans. Andrew Joron)

Andrea Applebee *Aletheia*

Eve Aschheim and Chris Daubert *Episodes with Wayne Thiebaud: Interviews*

Eve Aschheim *Eve Aschheim: Recent Work*

Anselm Berrigan *Pregrets*

Garrett Caples *The Garrett Caples Reader*

Marcel Cohen *Walls (Anamneses)* (trans. Brian Evenson and Joanna Howard)

Lynn Crawford *Fortification Resort*

Lynn Crawford *Simply Separate People, Two*

Thomas Devaney *You Are the Battery*

Ming Di (Editor) *New Poetry from China: 1917–2017* (trans. various)

Joseph Donahue *Red Flash on a Black Field*

Rachel Blau DuPlessis *Late Work*

Marcella Durand *To husband is to tender*

Rosalyn Drexler *To Smithereens*

Brian Evenson *Dark Property*

Serge Fauchereau *Complete Fiction* (trans. John Ashbery and Ron Padgett)

Jean Frémon *Painting* (trans. Brian Evenson)

Jean Frémon *The Paradoxes of Robert Ryman* (trans. Brian Evenson)

Ludwig Hohl *Ascent* (trans. Donna Stonecipher)

Isabelle Baladine Howald *phantomb* (trans. Eléna Rivera)

Philippe Jaccottet *Ponge, Pastures, Prairies* (trans. John Taylor)

Ann Jäderlund *Which once had been meadow* (trans. Johannes Göransson)

Franck André Jamme *Extracts from the Life of a Beetle* (trans. Michael Tweed)

Franck André Jamme *Another Silent Attack* (trans. Michael Tweed)

Franck André Jamme *The Recitation of Forgetting* (trans. John Ashbery)

Andrew Joron *Fathom*

Karl Larsson *FORM/FORCE* (trans. Jennifer Hayashida)

Hervé Le Tellier *Atlas Inutilis* (trans. Cole Swensen)

Eugene Lim *The Strangers*

Michael Leong *Cutting Time with a Knife*

Michael Leong *Words on Edge*

Gary Lutz *I Looked Alive*

Michèle Métail *Earth's Horizons: Panorama* (trans. Marcella Durand)

Michèle Métail *Identikits* (trans. Philip Terry)

Albert Mobilio *Me with Animal Towering*
Albert Mobilio *Touch Wood*
Albert Mobilio *Games & Stunts*
Albert Mobilio *Same Faces*
Pascalle Monnier *Bayart* (trans. Cole Swensen)
Christopher Nealon *The Joyous Age*
María Negroni *Berlin Interlude* (trans. Michelle Gil-Montero)
Doug Nufer *Never Again*
John Olson *Echo Regime*
John Olson *Free Stream Velocity*
Eva Kristina Olsson *The Angelgreen Sacrament* (trans. Johannes Göransson)
Juan Sánchez Peláez *Air on the Air: Selected Poems* (trans. Guillermo Parra)
Véronique Pittolo *Hero* (trans. Laura Mullen)
Pierre Reverdy *Prose Poems* (trans. Ron Padgett)
Pierre Reverdy *Haunted House* (trans. John Ashbery)
Pierre Reverdy *The Song of the Dead* (trans. Dan Bellm)
Pierre Reverdy *Georges Braque: A Methodical Adventure* (trans. Andrew Joron and
    Rose Vekony)
Valérie-Catherine Richez *THIS NOWHERE WHERE*
Barry Schwabsky *Book Left Open in the Rain*
Barry Schwabsky *Trembling Hand Equilibrium*
Barry Schwabsky *Heretics of Language*
Jeremy Sigler *Crackpot*
Jørn H. Sværen *Queen of England* (trans. Jørn H. Sværen)
Genya Turovskaya *The Breathing Body of This Thought*
Matvei Yankelevich *Some Worlds for Dr. Vogt*